The Scarlet Letter

紅字

Original Author   Nathaniel Hawthorne
Adaptor   Michael Robert Bradie
Illustrator   Julina Aleckcangra

WORDS
1000

MP3

Let's Enjoy Masterpieces!

All the beautiful fairy tales and masterpieces that you have encountered during your childhood remain as warm memories in your adulthood. This time, let's indulge in the world of masterpieces through English. You can enjoy the depth and beauty of original works, which you can't enjoy through Chinese translations.

The stories are easy for you to understand because of your familiarity with them. When you enjoy reading, your ability to understand English will also rapidly improve.

This series of *Let's Enjoy Masterpieces* is a special reading comprehension booster program, devised to improve reading comprehension for beginners whose command of English is not satisfactory, or who are elementary, middle, and high school students. With this program, you can enjoy reading masterpieces in English with fun and efficiency.

This carefully planned program is composed of 5 levels, from the beginner level of 350 words to the intermediate and advanced levels of 1,000 words. With this program's level-by-level system, you are able to read famous texts in English and to savor the true pleasure of the world's language.

The program is well conceived, composed of reader-friendly explanations of English expressions and grammar, quizzes to help the student learn vocabulary and understand the meaning of the texts, and fabulous illustrations that adorn every page. In addition, with our "Guide to Listening," not only is reading comprehension enhanced but also listening comprehension skills are highlighted.

In the audio recording of the book, texts are vividly read by professional American actors. The texts are rewritten, according to the levels of the readers by an expert editorial staff of native speakers, on the basis of standard American English with the ministry of education recommended vocabulary. Therefore, it will be of great help even for all the students that want to learn English.

Please indulge yourself in the fun of reading and listening to English through *Let's Enjoy Masterpieces*.

霍桑

Nathaniel Hawthorne
(1804-1864)

Nathaniel Hawthorne was an American novelist and short story writer. He was born into a strict Puritan family and liked to read as a child. After he graduated from college, he started to write stories for magazines in his hometown. His first novel was published in 1837 and gained him recognition as a serious writer. *The Scarlet Letter* was published in 1850.

Hawthorne is known as a writer who had an interest in human guilt and mental problems. In his writings he thoughtfully explored ideas about sin and the human conscience. He was especially interested in the Puritan traditions that he had grown up with and how these religious ideas interacted with the inner-descriptions, morality, religious beliefs, behavior, and psychological backgrounds of strict individuals. Hawthorne wrote about the people who suffered from religious guilt and people who became obsessed by solitude.

His best-known book is *The Scarlet Letter*. His other famous works include *Mosses from an Old Manse* (1846), *The House of the Seven Gables* (1851), *The Blithedale Romance* (1852), *Tanglewood Tales* (1853), and *The Marble Faun* (1860).

The Scarlet Letter is based on a love triangle between Hester Prynne, Arthur Dimmesdale, and Roger Chillingworth. This novel tells about the consequences of adultery in colonial Boston during the middle of 17th century. It carefully describes the sadness, solitude, and regrets of the characters, who are tortured by the conventional morality of the long-continued customs of their strict and severe Puritan society.

Hester Prynne, whose husband was presumed to have been lost at sea, lives alone in Boston. She becomes pregnant and gives birth to a daughter, whom she names Pearl. She is then publicly vilified and forced to wear the scarlet letter "A" on her clothing to indicate to everyone who meets her that she has committed the sin of adultery. But she refuses to reveal to anyone that her lover is Arthur Dimmesdale, the saintly young village minister.

Hester's husband, Roger Chillingworth, who has been away for a long time, reappears when Hester is in town to get her public punishment. Roger doesn't disclose his identity. He decides to discover who is Hester's lover. Roger will exact his revenge on the father of Pearl.

Feeling strong guilt for having committed adultery, young Arthur Dimmesdale becomes quite ill. He finally confesses to his adultery and dies in Hester's arms. In the end, Hester plans to take her daughter Pearl to Europe to begin a new life.

HOW TO USE THIS BOOK

本書使用說明

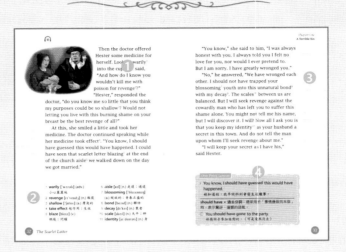

1 Original English texts

It is easy to understand the meaning of the text, because the text is rewritten according to the levels of the readers.

2 Explanation of the vocabulary

The words and expressions that include vocabulary above the elementary level are clearly defined.

3 Response notes

Spaces are included in the book so you can take notes about what you don't understand or what you want to remember.

4 One point lesson

In-depth analyses of major grammar points and expressions help you to understand sentences with difficult grammar.

🎧 Audio Recording

In the audio recording, native speakers narrate the texts in standard American English. By combining the written words and the audio recording, you can listen to English with great ease.

Audio books have been popular in Britain and America for many decades. They allow the listener to experience the proper word pronunciation and sentence intonation that add important meaning and drama to spoken English. Students will benefit from listening to the recording twenty or more times.

After you are familiar with the text and recording, listen once more with your eyes closed to check your listening comprehension. Finally, after you can listen with your eyes closed and understand every word and every sentence, you are then ready to mimic the native speaker.

Then you should make a recording by reading the text yourself. Then play both recordings to compare your oral skills with those of a native speaker.

HOW TO IMPROVE READING ABILITY

如何增進英文閱讀能力

① *Catch key words*

Read the key words in the sentences and practice catching the gist of the meaning of the sentence. You might question how working with a few important words could enhance your reading ability. However, it's quite effective. If you continue to use this method, you will find out that the key words and your knowledge of people and situations enables you to understand the sentence.

② *Divide long sentences*

Read in chunks of meaning, dividing sentences into meaningful chunks of information. In the book, chunks are arranged in sentences according to meaning. If you consider the sentences backwards or grammatically, your reading speed will be slow and you will find it difficult to listen to English.

You are ready to move to a more sophisticated level of comprehension when you find that narrowly focusing on chunks is irritating. Instead of considering the chunks, you will make it a habit to read the sentence from the beginning to the end to figure out the meaning of the whole.

③ Make inferences and assumptions

Making inferences and assumptions is part of your ability. If you don't know, try to guess the meaning of the words. Although you don't know all the words in context, don't go straight to the dictionary. Developing an ability to make inferences in the context is important.

The first way to figure out the meaning of a word is from its context. If you cannot make head or tail out of the meaning of a word, look at what comes before or after it. Ask yourself what can happen in such a situation. Make your best guess as to the word's meaning. Then check the explanations of the word in the book or look up the word in a dictionary.

④ Read a lot and reread the same book many times

There is no shortcut to mastering English. Only if you do a lot of reading will you make your way to the summit. Read fun and easy books with an average of less than one new word per page. Try to immerse yourself in English as often as you can.

Spend time "swimming" in English. Language learning research has shown that immersing yourself in English will help you improve your English, even though you may not be aware of what you're learning.

CONTENTS

Before You Read

Hester Prynne

I am a beautiful and independent woman, but my life is miserable and unlucky. I am married woman, but I had an affair with another man and had a baby. Now the townspeople[1] want me to tell them who the father of my child is! However, I will never tell. I will never betray[2] another person.

Reverend Dimmesdale

Oh, my life is wretched[3]! I tell people to behave properly[4], and to live according to God's will. They respect me despite[5] my youth. Yet, I am not worthy of their respect. I have a terrible secret that is burned upon the skin above my heart. Oh, how can I wash away my guilt and be free once more?

Pearl

While other children have a father, I don't! However, this does not bother me too much. I am free to play and do what I want most of the time. The adults[6] think that I have no manners[7], but they are all too serious and boring for me!

Roger Chillingworth

When I was away, my wife had a baby with another man. But I did not blame[8] her. She always told me that she did not love me. However, I do blame the father of the baby. I will find out who he is and punish him for his cowardly[9] silence.

Pastor John Wilson & Governor Bellingham

It is our duty[10] to make sure our Puritan[11] society lives according to the will of God. Hester Pyrnne must reveal[12] to us who the father of her child is. Only then will she be forgiven[13] by God.

1. **townspeople** [taʊnzpiːpəl] (n.)（總稱）市民；鎮民
2. **betray** [bɪ`treɪ] (v.) 背叛
3. **wretched** [`retʃɪd] (a.) 卑鄙的；無恥的
4. **properly** [`prɑːpərli] (adv.) 恰當地
5. **despite** [dɪ`spaɪt] (prep.) 儘管
6. **adult** [ə`dʌlt] (n.) 大人；成人

7. **manners** [`mænərz] (n.) 禮貌；規矩
8. **blame** [bleɪm] (v.) 責怪；指責
9. **cowardly** [`kaʊərdli] (a.) 懦弱的
10. **duty** [`duːti] (n.) 職責
11. **Puritan** [`pjʊrɪtən] (n.) 清教徒
12. **reveal** [rɪ`viːl] (v.) 揭露；透露
13. **forgive** [fər`giv] (v.) 寬恕；原諒（forgive-forgave-forgiven）

🎧 A Terrible Sin[1]

Although the forefathers[2] of the Boston Colony[3] strove[4] to create a utopian[5] society, two of the first things they built when they made their town were a cemetery[6] and a prison. On this day, twenty years after the first Puritan settlers[7] arrived in the New World colony, the townspeople gathered outside the prison.

"Good women," proclaimed[8] one woman, "if we judged wicked women like Hester Prynne, she would not have the easy sentence[9] that the town magistrates[10] have handed her!"

---

1. **sin** [sɪn] (n.) 罪惡；罪孽
2. **forefather** [ˋfɔːrˌfɑːðər] (n.) 祖先
3. **colony** [ˋkɑːləni] (n.) 殖民地
4. **strive** [straɪv] (v.) 努力；奮鬥 （strive-strove-striven）
5. **utopian** [juːˋtoupɪən] (a.) 烏托邦的；理想國的
6. **cemetery** [ˋsemәteri] (n.) 墓園；公墓（不屬於教會的）
7. **settler** [ˋsetlər] (n.) 殖民者；開拓者
8. **proclaim** [prouˋklem] (v.) 宣告；大聲說
9. **sentence** [ˋsentәns] (n.) 判定的刑罰

"Yes!" agreed another woman. "They should at least brand[11] the mark upon her forehead with a hot iron! By placing the mark on the front of her gown[12], she can cover it up anytime!"

"Yes!" cried another, "She may cover it as she likes, but the mark will always be on her heart!"

Then the prison door, covered in iron spikes[13], flew open. A large, frightening figure[14] in black came out from the inner darkness. With his hand, he tried to usher[15] out a young woman. But she pushed the hand away and stepped out into the open by her own free will, with an air of dignity[16].

10. **magistrate** [ˋmædʒɪstreɪt] (n.) 有司法權的行政長官；地方法官

11. **brand** [brænd] (v.) 烙印（於犯人、牲畜）；加諸污名

12. **gown** [gaʊn] (n.) 婦女禮服

13. **spike** [spaɪk] (n.) 長釘；尖鐵（尖頭朝上或朝內，用於防止侵入）

14. **figure** [ˋfɪgjər] (n.) 人影

15. **usher** [ˋʌʃər] (v.) 引導；引領

16. **dignity** [ˋdɪgnəti] (n.) 尊嚴

In the woman's arms was a three-month-old baby. The baby winked[1] because it was the first time it had ever felt sunlight on its face. The mother, standing fully revealed amid the townspeople, lowered[2] the baby in her arm to show her gown. She was blushing[3], but she wore a proud smile.

On the breast of her gown was a large letter A. The letter was made of fine, red cloth and embroidered[4] with rich, gold thread. The design was artistic and fanciful[5].

Hester Prynne was a tall young woman, with an elegant[6] figure and dark gleaming[7] hair. Those who knew her were amazed at her beauty and ladylike comportment[8] under these circumstances[9].

1. **wink** [wɪŋk] (v.) 眨眼
2. **lower** [`louər] (v.) 放低
3. **blush** [blʌʃ] (v.) 臉紅
4. **embroider** [ɪm`brɔɪdər] (v.) 刺繡
5. **fanciful** [`fænsɪfəl] (a.) 富於想像力的；別出心裁的
6. **elegant** [`elɪgənt] (a.) 高貴的；高雅的
7. **gleam** [gliːm] (v.) 發微光；閃爍
8. **comportment** [kəm`pourtmənt] (n.) 舉止；態度
9. **circumstances** [`sɜːrkəmˌstænsəz] (n.) 情況；環境
10. **sewing needle** [souɪŋ niːdl] (n.) 針黹；女紅
11. **remark** [rɪ`mɑːrk] (v.) 評論
12. **scarlet** [`skɑːrlɪt] (a.) 緋紅色的

"She certainly has great skill with the sewing needle[10]," remarked[11] one of the women, "but what a shameful way to show it!"

"Make way in the King's name!" shouted the prison officer. "Everyone will have a chance to get a good view of this wicked woman from now until noon. Come along, Hester. Show your scarlet[12] letter in the marketplace!"

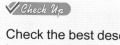

Check the best description of how Hester Prynne accepted her punishment.

a) With sorrow   b) With defiance   c) With shame

Ans: b

A lane opened up between the spectators[1], and Hester Prynne walked toward the area appointed[2] for public punishment. Calmly, she came to the scaffold[3] at the western end of the marketplace, next to Boston's oldest church.

The scaffold was a platform where punishments were carried out[4] publicly so as to impress the citizenry[5] into obeying the laws. There was a pillory[6] there, designed to hold a human head tightly and keep it in the public gaze. But Hester Prynne was not sentenced to its confinement[7]. Her sentence was just to stand on the platform for three hours.

1. **spectator** [`spekteɪtər] (n.)
   旁觀者；觀眾
2. **appointed** [ə`pɔɪntɪd] (a.)
   指定的
3. **scaffold** [`skæfəld] (n.)
   刑台
4. **carry out** 執行；實行
5. **citizenry** [`sɪtɪzənri] (n.)
   市民（集合名詞）
6. **pillory** [`pɪləri] (n.)
   示眾枷（一種刑具，用來夾罪犯的頭和手腕以示眾）
7. **confinement**
   [kən`faɪnmənt] (n.)
   限制；桎梏
8. **onlooker** [`ɑːn͵lukər] (n.)
   旁觀者；觀眾
9. **solemn** [`sɑːləm] (a.) 肅穆的

She climbed the steps and began her sentence. The onlookers[8] stared at her and the scarlet letter in solemn[9] silence. Hester had prepared herself to face the assault[10] of the public's scorn[11] and insults[12], but she found their heavy silence almost more difficult to bear.

When she stood there, her mind began to travel back into itself as memories began to surface[13]. She could see and feel the days of her happy childhood. Then she saw her face, gazing in the mirror, and its glow[14] of young beauty.

Then she saw the face of a man who was much older. His eyes were dim[15], and his skin was pale from many years of cloistered[16] study. His figure was slightly misshapen[17], his left shoulder a bit higher than his right.

✔Check Up Read the text and fill in blank.

Hester Prynne found it difficult to bear the townspeople's
_____.

Ans: silence

10. **assault** [ə`sɔːlt] (n.) 攻擊
11. **scorn** [skɔːrn] (n.) 蔑視；恥笑
12. **insult** [ɪn`sʌlt] (n.) 侮辱
13. **surface** [`sɜːrfɪs] (v.) 浮現
14. **glow** [gloʊ] (n.) 光輝；紅潤的氣色

15. **dim** [dɪm] (a.) 昏暗的；幽暗的
16. **cloistered** [`klɔɪstərd] (a.) 隱居的；埋頭專心研究的
17. **misshapen** [mɪs`ʃeɪpən] (a.) 畸型的；殘缺的

Then Hester Prynne's memories ended, and she found herself back on the scaffolding, surrounded by the townspeople. They were still staring at[1] her and the scarlet letter on her breast. She looked down at the letter on her chest and touched it to assure herself[2] it was real. And it was, as were the infant[3] and her burning shame.

After standing there for a little while, Hester saw a person on the edge of the crowd that she couldn't ignore[4]. He was a white man standing next to a native[5]. The white man, small, with a wrinkled[6] face, was wearing a mix of a civilized and savage costume[7].

Although he had tried to disguise[8] his physical[9] features[10], it was clear that his left shoulder was higher than his right. As she stared at him, her child cried in pain from the tightness of her grasp[11] on it, but she did not seem to hear.

1. **stare at** 盯視；凝視
2. **assure oneself**
   跟自己確定；保證
3. **infant** [ˋɪnfənt] (n.) 嬰兒
4. **ignore** [ɪgˋnɔːr] (v.) 忽視
5. **native** [ˋneɪtɪv] (n.)
   原住民；本地人
6. **wrinkled** [ˋrɪŋkəld] (a.)
   有皺紋的；皺的
7. **costume** [ˋkɑːstuːm] (n.)
   衣著；服裝

The man, who was a stranger in this town, stared back at Hester Prynne. At first his glance was careless, but as he began to understand the situation she was in, a look of horror came across his face.

Check Up True or False.

T F a The man with a native was a citizen of the town.

T F b The disguised man was not happy about Hester's situation.

Ans: a. F b. T

8. **disguise** [dɪs`gaɪz] (v.)
假扮；喬裝

9. **physical** [`fɪzɪkəl] (a.)
身體的；肉體的

10. **feature** [`fiːtʃər] (n.)
特徵；相貌

11. **grasp** [græsp] (n.) 抓；握

🎧 5

"I ask you, kind sir," the man said to a townsman, "Who is this woman, and why must she suffer[1] such public shame?"

"You must be a stranger to this town," answered the townsman. "Everyone who lives here knows about Hester Prynne and her wicked ways. She has created a huge scandal[2] among the members of Reverend[3] Dimmesdale's church."

"That's right," replied the man. "I am a stranger. I have been a captive[4] of the savage heathens[5] in the south for a long time. Please tell me of this woman Hester Prynne's crime."

"This woman is the wife of an English scholar. He decided to join our colony and sent his wife over ahead of him. But this man hasn't been heard from[6] in two years, and his young wife was left to her own poor judgment."

"Ah, I see what you mean," said the stranger with a bitter smile. "So who is the father of the baby she's holding?"

"That fact is the puzzling[7] question that remains for everyone," said the townsman. "Mrs. Prynne refuses to name the other sinner."

"Her husband should come and solve the mystery[8]," said the stranger.

1. **suffer** [`sʌfər] (v.)
   受苦；受罪
2. **scandal** [`skændəl] (n.) 醜聞
3. **reverend** [`revərənd] (n.)
   牧師（泛稱）
4. **captive** [`kæptɪv] (n.) 俘虜

5. **heathen** [`hiːðən] (n.)
   異教徒
6. **hear from sb** 有某人的音訊
7. **puzzling** [`pʌzlɪŋ] (a.)
   令人困惑的
8. **mystery** [`mɪstəri] (n.) 謎團

    "Yes, he should if he's still alive," agreed the townsman. "The penalty[1] for this crime is normally death, but the magistrates were merciful[2] because her husband is probably at the bottom of the sea. But afterward she will bear the scarlet mark of an adulterer[3] for the rest of her life."

    "It is a wise punishment," said the stranger. "Her mark will serve as[4] a living sermon[5] against sin. But it angers me that her fellow[6] sinner is not standing there next to her. But he will be discovered and known. He will!"

    As the stranger walked away, Hester Prynne kept her eyes on[7] him. She was relieved[8] to be in the presence of the crowd so as not to meet the man alone.

---

1. **penalty** [`penəlti] (n.)
   刑罰；罪刑
2. **merciful** [`mɜːrsɪfəl] (a.)
   仁慈的
3. **adulterer** [ə`dʌltərər] (n.)
   通姦者
4. **serve as** . . . 當作……
5. **sermon** [`sɜːrmən] (n.) 佈道
6. **fellow** [`felou] (a.) 共事的

7. **keep one's eyes on**
   緊盯著……
8. **relieved** [rɪ`liːvd] (a.)
   鬆了一口氣的
9. **balcony** [`bælkəni] (n.) 露台
10. **pronounce** [prə`nauns] (n.)
    宣佈
11. **governor** [`gʌvənər] (n.)
    美國的州長；市長

Suddenly, she was awoken from her thoughts by a voice, "Hester Prynne, you must now listen to me!" Standing on the balcony[9] of the nearby church, used by magistrates to pronounce[10] sentences, was Governor[11] Bellingham. There were other noblemen on the balcony with the governor and his men.

Hester Prynne faced the balcony. The voice she had heard belonged to Boston's oldest minister[12], Pastor[13] John Wilson.

---

12. **minister** [ˋmɪnɪstər] (n.)
    神職人員；英國國教之外的新
    教牧師（尤指長老教會的）

13. **pastor** [ˋpæstər] (n.)
    主管教堂的牧師；
    英國國教之外的新教牧師

"Hester Prynne," continued the old pastor, "I have told your minister here, the Reverend Mr. Dimmesdale, that he should force you to tell us the name of the wicked man who had tempted[1] you to this sad fall here and now[2]."

Then Governor Bellingham spoke, "Good Reverend Dimmesdale, as her minister, you are responsible for this woman's soul. You must urge[3] her to speak and therefore prove her repentance[4]."

To respond, Reverend Dimmesdale rose to address the crowd. The reverend was a young clergyman[5] who had graduated from one of the great English universities. His powerful voice and impressive intellect[6] had already brought him great respect and admiration from the colonists[7] he served.

1. **temp** [temp] (v.) 引誘；誘惑
2. **here and now** 當下；立刻
3. **urge** [ɜːrdʒ] (v.) 敦促；力勸
4. **repentance** [rɪˋpentəns] (n.) 懺悔；悔悟
5. **clergyman** [ˋklɜːrdʒimən](n.) （美國）泛指一般神職人員； （英國國教）主教以外的牧師
6. **intellect** [ˋɪntəlekt] (n.) 智識；才智
7. **colonist** [ˋkɑːlənɪst] (n.) 殖民地居民（尤指殖民地開拓者）
8. **misplaced** [mɪsˋpleɪst] (a.) 寄託錯的
9. **affect** [əˋfekt] (v.) 影響
10. **entreaty** [ɪnˋtriːti] (n.) 懇求

"Speak to the woman, brother," urged Pastor Wilson. "You are the only one who can save her soul!"

Reverend Dimmesdale looked to the woman on the scaffolding. "Hester Prynne," he began. "You've heard what the good Pastor Wilson has said. I urge you to speak the name of your fellow sinner. It will give both of your hearts peace. Do not remain silent out of misplaced[8] pity or tenderness for him!"

Even the baby in Hester Prynne's arms was affected[9] by the reverend's powerful voice. It looked up at him with a half-happy, half-sad expression on its face. But to this entreaty[10], Hester just shook her head.

✓ Check Up

What does Hester Prynne have to do in order to save her soul?
- a She must give up her baby to the true father.
- b She must marry the father of her baby.
- c She must tell the townspeople who the father of her baby is.

Ans: c

"Woman, do not test the limits of Heaven's mercy!" said Pastor Wilson with an angry voice. "Speak the name, and your repentance will be enough to take the scarlet letter off your breast!"

1. **remove** [rɪ`muːv] (v.)
   除去；移除
2. **endure** [ɪn`dʊr] (v.) 忍受
3. **agony** [`ægəni] (n.)
   （精神或肉體）極大的痛苦
4. **stern** [stɜːrn] (a.)
   嚴峻的；冷酷的
5. **earthly** [`ɜːrθli] (a.) 凡塵的
6. **heavenly** [`hevənli] (a.)
   天堂的；天國的
7. **confess** [kən`fes] (v.)
   坦承；告白
8. **lean** [liːn] (v.)
   傾身（向前或向後）

"Never!" shouted Hester Prynne. She looked deeply into Reverend Dimmesdale's eyes. "This letter is branded too deeply on my heart to remove[1] it so easily. I hope to endure[2] his agony[3] as well as my own!"

"Speak!" cried the townspeople around the scaffolding. "Speak the name of your baby's father!"

She went pale as she seemed to recognize one of the stern[4], cold voices coming from the crowd. But she insisted, "I will not speak. My baby will never have an earthly[5] father. She will have to know the heavenly[6] one!"

"She won't confess[7] his name," whispered Dimmesdale, as he leaned[8] over the balcony with his hand over his heart. "She will not speak!" he announced to the crowd.

One Point Lesson

I hope to endure his agony as well as my own!
我希望能把他的痛苦，連同自己的痛苦，一併承受下來！

1. **A as well as B**：這個句型結構中，在意義上重點放在 A，因此以 A 為主詞的述語動詞的單複數，應與 A 符合。

2. **as well as** 的意思有：
   (1) 與……一樣好 (2) 不但……而且…… (3) 也；以及

   e.g. I hate you as well as your father.
   我恨妳，也恨妳父親。

   e.g. Mary, as well as her parents, is late.
   瑪麗和她的父母都遲到了。

Once Hester had returned to the prison, she was in a state of nervous hysteria[1]. And the baby kept crying wildly. Master Brackett, the jailer[2], kept a constant[3] watch on her to make sure she did not hurt herself or her baby. Finally, he brought in a doctor to see her. The doctor was the same stranger who had taken an interest in her while she had been on the scaffolding. His name was Roger Chillingworth.

As the jailer led him into the room and Hester Prynne saw him, she became as still as death.

"Don't worry," the doctor told the jailer. "I'll take great care of Mrs. Prynne and her child. You will soon have peace and quiet in your prison."

The doctor mixed up[4] an herbal[5] remedy[6] from local plants that he had learned from the natives.

---

1. **hysteria** [hɪˋstɪrɪə] (n.) 歇斯底里
2. **jailer** [ˋdʒeɪlər] (n.) 獄卒
3. **constant** [ˋkɑːnstənt] (a.) 持續不斷的
4. **mix up** 摻和；調製
5. **herbal** [ˋhɜːrbəl] (a.) 草藥的
6. **remedy** [ˋremədi] (n.) 藥物
7. **avenge** [əˋvendʒ] (v.) 為……報仇

8. **soothing** [ˋsuːðɪŋ] (a.) 安撫的
9. **misbegotten** [ˌmɪsbɪˋgɑːtn] (a.) 私生的
10. **hesitantly** [ˋhɛzətəntli] (adv.) 猶豫地
11. **drop off to sleep** 一下子就睡了

"Here Mrs. Prynne, give this to your baby. She'll only accept it from your hands, and it will calm her."

Hester pushed his hand away. "Would you avenge yourself[7] by poisoning this innocent baby?" she whispered.

"Woman, don't be foolish!" the doctor responded in a cold yet soothing[8] manner. "I would not harm this poor, misbegotten[9] baby."

Hesitantly[10], she gave the drink to her infant, and it dropped peacefully off to sleep[11].

✔ *Check Up* Fill in the blank.

The doctor gave an _____ drink to Hester to make her baby sleep.

Ans: herbal

31

Then the doctor offered Hester some medicine for herself. Looking warily[1] into the cup, she said, "And how do I know you wouldn't kill me with poison for revenge[2]?"

"Hester," responded the doctor, "do you know me so little that you think my purposes could be so shallow[3]? Would not letting you live with this burning shame on your breast be the best revenge of all?"

At this, she smiled a little and took her medicine. The doctor continued speaking while her medicine took effect[4]. "You know, I should have guessed this would have happened. I could have seen that scarlet letter blazing[5] at the end of the church aisle[6] we walked down on the day we got married."

1. **warily** [`wɛrəli] (adv.)
   小心翼翼地
2. **revenge** [rɪ`vendʒ] (n.) 報復
3. **shallow** [`ʃælou] (a.) 膚淺的
4. **take effect** 起作用；生效
5. **blaze** [bleɪz] (v.)
   燃燒；閃耀
6. **aisle** [aɪl] (n.) 走道；通道
7. **blossoming** [`blɑ:səmɪŋ]
   (a.) 綻放的；青春正盛的
8. **bond** [bɑ:nd] (n.) 聯結
9. **decay** [dɪ`keɪ] (n.) 衰老
10. **scale** [skeɪl] (n.) 天平；秤
11. **identity** [aɪ`dentəti] (n.) 身分

"You know," she said to him, "I was always honest with you. I always told you I felt no love for you, nor would I ever pretend to. But I am sorry. I have greatly wronged you."

"No," he answered, "We have wronged each other. I should not have trapped your blossoming[7] youth into this unnatural bond[8] with my decay[9]. The scales[10] between us are balanced. But I will seek revenge against the cowardly man who has left you to suffer this shame alone. You might not tell me his name, but I will discover it. I will! Now all I ask you is that you keep my identity[11] as your husband a secret in this town. And do not tell the man upon whom I'll seek revenge about me."

"I will keep your secret as I have his," said Hester.

One Point Lesson

- You know, I **should have guessed** this would have happened.
  妳知道的，我早該料到會發生這種事。

---

should have + 過去分詞：通常用於「事情應做而未做」時，表示驚訝、遺憾的語氣。

- You **should have gone** to the party.
  妳應該去參加派對的。（可是竟然沒去）

A Match the names with the character descriptions.

① Hester Prynne   •

② Pastor Wilson   •

③ Roger Chillingworth   •

④ Governor Bellingham   •

⑤ Reverend Dimmesdale   •

• ⓐ the man Hester Prynne married

• ⓑ a magistrate in Boston colony

• ⓒ the oldest minister in Boston colony

• ⓓ a handsome young minister with a powerful voice

• ⓔ a tall woman with an elegant figure

B Select the ones that use the underlined words correctly.

① (a) She <u>gathered</u> a scarlet letter on her breast.
   (b) The townspeople <u>gathered</u> outside the prison.

② (a) The baby <u>ushered</u> when it saw the sunlight.
   (b) With his hand, he tried to <u>usher</u> out a young woman.

③ (a) That fact is the <u>puzzling</u> question that remains for everyone.
   (b) The old man was <u>puzzling</u> a look in her eye.

C Choose the best answer to each question.

1 What did the scarlet A on Hester Prynne's bosom stand for?

(a) Alphabet   (b) Adulterer   (c) Admirable

2 What fact did Roger Chillingworth make Hester Prynne swear to conceal?

(a) That he was not a real doctor.

(b) That he was the father of her baby.

(c) That he was her husband.

D Fill in the blanks with the given words.

fanciful   merciful   sermon   spikes   misbegotten

1 Her mark will serve as a living _____ against sin.

2 Then the prison door, covered in iron _____, flew open.

3 The design was artistic and _____.

4 The penalty for this crime is normally death, but the magistrates were _____.

5 I would not harm this poor, _____ baby.

Chapter Two

🎧 Hester's Pearl

The imprisonment[1] of Hester Prynne ended shortly after her discussion with the doctor, but the torment[2] of her life among the townspeople was just beginning.

She was free to leave the town. But Hester had decided to stay and face her lifelong sentence. She and her baby moved into a small cottage[3] on the outskirts[4] of town. She was able to make a decent[5] living with her expert sewing[6] skills. But she spent very little of her income on herself. She dressed her young daughter very well and gave her extra money to charity[7].

---

1. **imprisonment** [ɪmˈprɪzənmənt] (n.) 監禁
2. **torment** [ˈtɔːrment] (n.) 折磨;煎熬
3. **cottage** [ˈkɑːtɪdʒ] (n.) 木屋;農舍
4. **outskirt** [ˈaʊtskɜːrt] (n.) 〔常用複數〕郊區

5. **decent** [ˈdiːsənt] (a.) 正派的;像樣的
6. **sewing** [ˈsoʊɪŋ] (n.) 縫紉
7. **charity** [ˈtʃærəti] (n.) 慈善活動(機構)
8. **hire** [haɪr] (v.) 僱用;租用
9. **perceive** [pərˈsiːv] (v.) 察覺;看出

Because of her exceptional skill, the townspeople always hired[8] Hester to do work. But they never allowed her to forget her shame with their looks and words.

Hester's daughter, Pearl, had been named not for a pearl's great beauty or value, but rather for its great price.

Nevertheless, the baby soon blossomed into a beautiful but strange child. When Hester watched her daughter and perceived[9] the young girl's strange behavior, she worried that the child was somehow also connected and influenced by the scarlet letter.

✓ Check Up

How did Hester Prynne make a living?

- a She took care of some young girls from the town.
- b She worked as a seamstress.
- c She sold pearls that she found on the beach.

As Pearl got older, it became clear that the child could not be forced to adapt[1] to rules. She would not heed[2] the simplest of her mother's commands[3]. And her temper were uneven[4]. It was as if the warfare[5] of Hester's spirit[6] were carrying on[7] in Pearl.

Hester would have liked to see her playing with other children. But Pearl was as much an outcast[8] as her mother, and she accepted her position from the time when she was very young.

Fate had built an unbreakable wall around Pearl. When she did meet some of the town's vicious[9] Puritan children, who gathered around her, she would become terrible, flinging[10] stones at them and screaming like a small savage.

The sight of her combative[11] daughter brought Hester to her knees, asking, "Dear Heavenly Father, what kind of being is this that I've brought into the world?"

---

1. **adapt** [əˋdæpt] (v.) 適應
2. **heed** [hiːd] (v.) 注意
3. **command** [kəˋmænd] (n.) 吩咐
4. **uneven** [ʌnˋiːvən] (a.) 起伏不平的
5. **warfare** [ˋwɔːrfer] (n.) 戰爭
6. **spirit** [ˋspɪrɪt] (n.) 靈魂；精神
7. **carry on** 繼續
8. **outcast** [ˋaʊtkæst] (n.) 被驅逐的人
9. **vicious** [ˋvɪʃəs] (a.) 惡毒的
10. **fling** [flɪŋ] (v.) 扔；擲 （fling-flung-flung）
11. **combative** [kəmˋbætɪv] (a.) 好鬥的
12. **elf** [elf] (n.) 小精靈
13. **intelligence** [ɪnˋtelɪdʒəns] (n.) 智能
14. **bosom** [ˋbuzəm] (n.) 胸部

And when little Pearl heard her mother cry like this, she would merely look at her and smile with her elf[12]-like intelligence[13].

One of the strangest things about Pearl was that as a baby, her first interest had not been her mother's smile, as it is with most infants. Rather her first attraction was to the scarlet A on her mother's bosom[14].

It was **as if** the warfare of Hester's spirit **were** carrying on in Pearl.
就彷彿賀絲特靈魂裡的戰爭，在珍珠的身上延燒著。

as if + 子句：假設句，表示子句所述「彷彿為真」。

e.g. It seemed **as if** I **were** dreaming.
（那情況）彷彿是我在作夢一樣。

🎧 13

Some years later, Pearl was running around. One day, she gathered a bundle[1] of wildflowers. She then began pitching[2] them at the letter on her mother's breast and dancing up and down with joy when one of them hit the scarlet letter.

1. **bundle** [`bʌndl] (n.) 束；綑
2. **pitch** [pɪtʃ] (v.) 投；擲
3. **instinct** [`ɪnstɪŋkt] (n.) 本能；直覺力
4. **penance** [`penəns] (n.) 贖罪的苦行
5. **flash** [flæʃ] (v.) 閃爍；閃現
6. **demonic** [dɪ`mɑːnɪk] (a.) 惡魔似的
7. **pause** [pɔːz] (n.) 短暫停頓
8. **keen** [kiːn] (a.) 敏銳的
9. **shudder** [`ʃʌdər] (v.) 發抖；戰慄

Hester's first instinct[3] was to cover the letter with her arms. But she resisted, considering each flower's painful strike against her heart to be part of her penance[4]. To her mother's obvious pain, Pearl only laughed, her eyes flashing[5] with a demonic[6] glow.

"Are you really my child?" Hester asked her playfully. "Who made you, and who sent you here?"

"You tell me," replied Pearl, who became very serious. "Do tell me."

"The Heavenly Father sent you," Hester answered after a pause[7].

But her hesitation was not lost on the child's keen[8] intelligence.

"He did not send me," cried Pearl. "I have no Heavenly Father!"

"Oh please," cried Hester. "You mustn't say that. He created all of us!"

"No, you must tell me," laughed Pearl, who danced about. "Do tell me!"

Hester shuddered[9], unable to answer her question.

One day, Hester brought Pearl with her to Governor Bellingham's mansion[1]. She told Pearl they were going to return a pair of gloves he had asked her to embroider, but the real reason was that Hester had heard rumors that the townspeople were planning to take her daughter away from her.

They suspected Pearl might be a demon[2] child, so by taking her away, they planned to save Hester's soul. Hester had also heard that Governor Bellingham was at the head of[3] this plan.

1. **mansion** [ˈmænʃən] (n.) 大宅邸
2. **demon** [ˈdiːmən] (n.) 惡魔
3. **at the head of** 主持；首腦
4. **extension** [ɪkˈstenʃən] (n.) 延伸

5. **luxurious** [lʌgˈʒuriəs] (a.) 奢侈的
6. **rosebush** [ˈrozbuʃ] (n.) 玫瑰樹叢
7. **demand** [dɪˈmænd] (v.) 要求

So she made up her mind to speak with him.

That day, she had dressed Pearl in a bright red dress that was embroidered with gold thread, just like her scarlet A, so that the child seemed to be a living extension[4] of it.

When they reached the luxurious[5] mansion, Pearl saw a blossoming rosebush[6] and demanded[7] that her mother pick one of the red flowers for her.

✓ *Check Up* True or False.

T F a Hester suspected that the Governor planned to take Pearl away from her.

T F b Hester went to the Governor's mansion to return a pair of gloves.

Ans: a.T b.F

15

When Hester refused, Pearl burst into[1] a fit[2] of tears and let out an ear-piercing[3] scream. But she then suddenly became silent when she saw some people approaching[4] them.

In the group were Governor Bellingham, Pastor Wilson, the young Reverend Arthur Dimmesdale, and Doctor Roger Chillingworth. Reverend Dimmesdale's health had been suffering as of late, and the doctor, who was treating[5] him, had become his close and constant companion.

Looking with surprise at the little girl dressed in stunning[6] scarlet, the governor asked, "Who is this little one here?"

"Ah, this is the daughter of the unfortunate Hester Prynne," Pastor Wilson said. "She is the one we've spoken about recently."

"Yes," said Governor Bellingham.

1. **burst into . . .** 猛然……
   （burst-burst-burst）
2. **fit** [fɪt] (n.)
   （感情等的）突發
3. **piercing** [`pɪrsɪŋ] (a.)
   刺耳的
4. **approach** [ə`proutʃ] (v.)
   接近；來到近前
5. **treat** [triːt] (v.)
   治療；以醫術照顧
6. **stunning** [`stʌnɪŋ] (a.)
   極亮麗的
7. **eternal** [ɪ`tɜːrnəl] (a.)
   永恆的
8. **clothe** [kloʊð] (v.) 著衣

"We shall look into this matter right here and now. Hester Prynne," he said, looking directly at the letter on her breast, "we have greatly discussed as to whether it is our duty to protect the eternal[7] souls of you and your child. Don't you think it would be best for this child to be taken and clothed[8] plainly[9] and disciplined[10] in the truths of Heaven and Earth?"

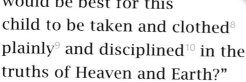

"I can teach my daughter better than anyone else," said Hester Prynne, putting her finger on her letter. "I have learned from this."

"Woman," said the governor, "that is your badge[11] of shame, and the reason we think it best to put the child in more righteous[12] hands."

9. **plainly** [ˈpleɪnli] (adv.)
   樸素地

10. **discipline** [ˈdɪsəplɪn] (v.)
    教導；管教

11. **badge** [bædʒ] (n.)
    徽章；標記

12. **righteous** [ˈraɪtʃəs] (a.)
    有德的；廉正的

16

"Nevertheless," Hester Prynne said calmly, "it has taught me lessons which will make my daughter wiser and better."

"We will be the judges of that," said Bellingham. Then he sat down in a chair and tried to put Pearl between his knees, but the child, unaccustomed to[1] the touch of anyone but her mother, escaped[2].

---

1. **unaccustomed to . . .**
   不習慣於……
2. **escape** [ɪˋskeɪp] (v.) 逃脫
3. **examination**
   [ɪɡˏzæmɪˋneɪʃən] (n.)
   審問；查問
4. **belief** [bɪˋliːf] (n.)
   信仰；信念

5. **creation** [kriˋeɪʃən] (n.)
   創造
6. **mischievously**
   [ˋmɪstʃɪvəsli] (adv.) 惡作劇地
7. **pluck** [plʌk] (v.) 摘下；拔出
8. **grab** [ɡræb] (v.) 抓住
9. **torture** [ˋtɔːrtʃər] (n.) 折磨

Pastor Wilson, who was known to be good with children, continued the examination[3], "Pearl, can you tell me who made you?"

Hester Prynne had educated her child at home in the matters of Puritan beliefs[4] about the creation[5] of the human spirit. But Pearl decided to answer the serious question mischievously[6]. She then announced that she had not been made in Heaven, but rather she had been plucked[7] from the wild rosebush that grew by the prison door.

"This is terrible," the governor cried. "Here is a three-year-old child who can't tell who made her!"

Hester Prynne grabbed[8] Pearl into her arms, "God gave me this child in return for all the things he has taken from me. She is my happiness and my torture[9]! I will die before you take her from me!"

"Child," said old Pastor Wilson, "Pearl will be cared for better than you can do!"

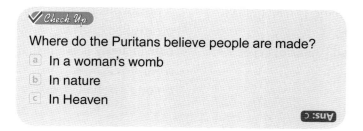

Check Up

Where do the Puritans believe people are made?
- a In a woman's womb
- b In nature
- c In Heaven

Ans: c

17

"God gave her to me for safekeeping[1]!" screamed Hester Prynne. Then she turned to the young Reverend Dimmesdale and cried, "You speak for me! You were my pastor and in charge of my soul! You know me better than these men can! Don't let them take her away from me!"

"There is truth in her words," Reverend Dimmesdale said in his powerful, trembling[2] voice. "God gave this child to this mother to teach her to change her wicked ways. That bond is sacred[3]. Who are we to say that God made a mistake in giving the child to her? Who are we to take away the good Lord's one blessing[4] in her life?"

"Well spoken," said Pastor Wilson. "What do you say, Governor Bellingham? The good reverend has pleaded[5] convincingly[6] on Hester Prynne's behalf[7]."

---

1. **safekeeping** [ˌseɪfˋkiːpɪŋ] (n.) 妥善保管
2. **trembling** [ˋtrɛmblɪŋ] (a.) 顫抖的
3. **sacred** [ˋseɪkrɪd] (a.) 神聖的
4. **blessing** [ˋblesɪŋ] (n.) 賜福
5. **plead** [pliːd] (v.) 答辯；辯護（plead-pleaded-pleaded / plead-pled-pled）
6. **convincingly** [kənˋvɪnsɪŋli] (adv.) 令人信服地
7. **on one's behalf** 代表某人

"Indeed he has," answered the governor.

"Pearl shall stay with her mother, and we will make no further scandal of the matter. At the proper time, the church's officers will make sure that she goes to school and church. That's all."

Then young Pearl grabbed Reverend Dimmesdale's hand and put it on her cheek. The minister looked around and then kissed her forehead.

✔ Check Up

What did Reverend Dimmesdale NOT say about why Hester should keep Pearl?

a. Pearl is the one blessing in Hester's life.
b. There is a sacred bond between a mother and her daughter.
c. Hester can teach Pearl better than anyone else can.

Ans: c

18

"A strange child," said Doctor Chillingworth. "Perhaps if we study her nature, we'll be able to guess the identity of her sinful father."

"It would be sinful to do that," answered Pastor Wilson. "It would be better to pray on the matter and leave it to God's will."

1. **settle** [`setl] (v.) 解決
2. **execute** [`eksɪkjuːt] (v.) 處死
3. **practice** [`præktɪs] (v.) 實施
4. **witchcraft** [`wɪtʃkræft] (n.) 巫術
5. **hiss** [hɪs] (v.) 發出嘶嘶聲；發出噓聲

After the matter was settled[1], Hester Prynne and Pearl left the governor's mansion. Outside the house they met Mistress Hibbins, Governor Bellingham's bitter sister, who was executed[2] a few years later for practicing[3] witchcraft[4].

"Hst hst," she hissed[5]. "Will you two come with us to the forest tonight to hold congregation[6] with the Black Man?"

"We will not!" answered Hester Prynne. "I will stay at home with my daughter. But if they had taken her from me, I would have come with you and signed my name in the evil Black Man's[7] book in my own blood!"

After this, it could be said that even this early, the child had saved Hester Prynne's soul from Satan's[8] trap.

6. **congregation**
   [ˌkɑːŋerɪˈɡeɪʃən] (n.) 集會
7. **the Black Man** 惡魔；撒旦

8. **Satan** [ˈseɪtn] (n.)
   撒旦；魔鬼

 Check Up

How did Pearl save her mother's soul?
- a Pearl taught Hester about God's forgiveness.
- b Pearl was the reason Hester did not join Mistress Hibbins.
- c Pearl convinced her mother to sign her name in the Black Man's book.

Ans: b

About Puritans and Pilgrim

Most American high school students learn that the first Pilgrims[1] came from England, and this is true to a certain degree. Most of these Pilgrims actually came from Holland, where they lived for a while after leaving England.

The Pilgrims were Puritans who believed that everyone should be highly educated, and that any one of their members could be elected[2] to high positions in the church. The English monarchy[3] did not like these ideas, as they were actually similar to a democratic[4] form of government.

However, the Puritans were not political. They were more interested in living according to their strict and pure religion. The Puritans left England for Holland, but they did not like living there, either. They were afraid that the Dutch influence would corrupt[5] weaker members of their Puritan community.

They wanted to live in a remote[6] area, where they would be free not only to live their lives as they saw fit, but also to control others and to force them to live a strict Puritan lifestyle also. They were successful in creating this type of society after coming to the New World, and this is the setting for the *Scarlet Letter*.

Actually, their ideas served as some of the basic, founding ideas of the American nation many, many years after the Pilgrims arrived in the New World.

---

1. **the Pilgrims**（P 大寫）此處特指移民新大陸的清教徒
2. **elect** [ɪ`lekt] (v.) 選舉
3. **monarchy** [`mɑ:nərki] (n.) 君主政權
4. **democratic** [ˌdemə`krætɪk] (a.) 民主的
5. **corrupt** [kə`rʌpt] (v.) 腐敗；腐化
6. **remote** [rɪ`mout] (a.) 偏僻的；僻遠的

⌂19 Revenge

It was around the time that Roger Chillingworth settled in the town as a doctor that the young Reverend Dimmesdale's health began to decline[1]. The townspeople saw the coincidence[2] of the ailing[3] reverend and the doctor's arrival as a miracle enacted[4] by the providence[5] of God. Therefore the town elders thought it was God's will that reverend Dimmesdale's health be placed in Dr. Chillingworth's hands. The two men soon became constant companions.

---

1. **decline** [dɪˋklaɪn] (v.) 衰退
2. **coincidence** [koʊˋɪnsɪdəns] (n.) 巧合
3. **ailing** [ˋeɪlɪŋ] (a.) 生病的
4. **enact** [ɪˋnækt] (v.) 上演;執行
5. **providence** [ˋprɑːvɪdəns] (n.) 天意

Reverend Dimmesdale was fascinated[6] by Chillingworth's wealth of experience as a doctor and an older man, while the doctor spent his time looking for clues to the reverend's illness. Chillingworth was convinced[7] that his bodily sickness was the result of a troubled heart and mind. Yet the doctor was unable to figure out[8] just what was troubling the reverend's mind.

The two men soon moved into a house together. But as time passed, the townspeople began to see Doctor Chillingworth differently. His appearance and demeanor[9] had changed remarkably since moving to the town.

Where he was once calm and kind, they now saw evil on his face. Rumors around town said that the reverend's poor health was caused by Satan, who haunted[10] him in the form of Roger Chillingworth.

---

6. **fascinated** [ˈfæsɪneɪtɪd]
   (a.) 著迷的
7. **convinced** [kənˈvɪnst] (a.)
   確信的
8. **figure out** 弄清楚
9. **demeanor** [dɪˈmiːnər] (n.)
   舉止；態度
10. **haunt** [hɔːnt] (v.) 纏住

It happened one day that the reverend visited Chillingworth in his laboratory[1], where he often made drugs from plants he had collected. The doctor was examining a bundle of ugly-looking plants from the graveyard[2] that stood next to their house.

"I found these leaves in that graveyard right there," said the doctor, pointing out the window. "This variety is new to me. I found them growing out of an unmarked grave. I suspect they grew out of the man's heart. Perhaps they represent a dreadful secret that he was buried with. It would have been better that he confessed it during his lifetime."

"Maybe he wanted to but was unable," said the reverend, gripping[3] his breast as if it were throbbing[4] with pain. "When the members of my church confess their sins, they are always greatly relieved."

---

1. **laboratory** [`læbrətɔːri] (n.) 實驗室
2. **graveyard** [`greɪvjɑːrd] (n.) 墓地
3. **grip** [grɪp] (v.) 緊握
4. **throb** [θrɑːb] (v.) 悸動；心怦怦跳
5. **footpath** [`fʊtpæθ] (n.) 小徑；步道
6. **disrespectfully** [ˌdɪsrɪ`spɛktfəli] (adv.) 無禮地
7. **skip** [skɪp] (v.) 輕快地跳躍
8. **prickly** [`prɪkli] (a.) 有刺的
9. **burr** [bɜːr] (n.) 有芒刺的果實
10. **burdock** [`bɜːrdɑːk] (n.) 牛蒡
11. **stick** [stɪk] (v.) 黏附 （stick-stuck-stuck）

Just then the doctor and the reverend saw
Hester Prynne and Pearl walking over a
footpath[5] that ran through the graveyard. Pearl
was disrespectfully[6] skipping[7] along from the
top of one tomb to the next. Then she
gathered a handful of prickly[8] burrs[9] from a
burdock[10] plant and stuck[11] them along the
lines of her mother's scarlet A.

✔ *Check Up* Fill in the blank.

He would not _____ his mistake, even though
everyone knew he was guilty of it.

Ans: confess

"Ah, that child has no respect for law or authority[1]," said Roger Chillingworth. "Just the other day I saw her splash[2] water from a horse trough[3] on the governor. What in Heaven's name is wrong with her?"

Suddenly, Pearl ran up to the window and threw one of the prickly burrs at Reverend Dimmesdale. Then she laughed and called to her mother, "Let's go, Mother. Or the Black Man is going to get you like he has already gotten the reverend. Come quickly, or he'll catch you! But he can't catch me!"

"Do you think Hester Prynne is less miserable for bearing her shame in that letter on her breast, rather than hiding it away in her heart?" the doctor asked the reverend as the mother and her child walked away from the window.

"Yes, I believe so," answered the reverend. "But what I really want to talk about right now is my health. What is your judgment as to the cause of my chronic[4] ailment[5]?"

"Frankly speaking[6]," said the doctor, "I want to know if you have any secrets you're failing to tell me. Have you told me everything about your problems?"

1. **authority** [ə`θɔːrɪti] (n.)
   權威
2. **splash** [splæʃ] (v.) 潑；濺
3. **trough** [trɑːf] (n.)
   水槽；食槽
4. **chronic** [`krɑːnɪk] (a.)
   慢性病的；痼疾的

5. **ailment** [`eɪlmənt] (n.)
   （輕微或慢性的）疾病；
   （生理或心理的）失調
6. **frankly speaking**
   坦白說

✔ Check Up

What did Pearl accuse the reverend of?
a Having no respect for authority
b Bearing shame in his heart
c Being caught by the Black Man

Ans: c

This probing[1] line of questioning visibly flustered[2] the reverend. "But . . . of course I have," he stammered[3]. "Of course there are parts of my soul I could never expose to an Earthly doctor."

"But how can I cure your body if you have not laid open your mind and soul?"

At this, the reverend suddenly became fiercely[4] angry and shoved[5] the doctor's hands away from him. With a frantic[6] gesture, he stormed out of the room.

Within a couple of hours, the reverend returned to the doctor's laboratory and apologized for his outburst[7]. The two resumed[8] their friendship effortlessly.

But later that day, while the reverend slept in his chair, the doctor crept[9] silently into his room. Putting his hand on the sleeping man's chest, the doctor pushed back the reverend's shirt and looked at his bare chest.

---

1. **probe** [proʊb] (v.) 刺探
2. **fluster** [ˋflʌstər] (v.) 慌張
3. **stammer** [ˋstæmər] (v.) 結結巴巴地說
4. **fiercely** [ˋfɪrsli] (adv.) 激烈地
5. **shove** [ʃʌv] (v.) 推；撞
6. **frantic** [ˋfræntɪk] (a.) 發狂似的
7. **outburst** [ˋaʊtbɜːrst] (n.) 發脾氣
8. **resume** [rɪˋzuːm] (v.) 恢復
9. **creep** [kriːp] (v.) 悄悄地靠近 （creep-crept-crept）
10. **devilish** [ˋdevəlɪʃ] (a.) 如魔鬼的
11. **subtly** [ˋsʌtli] (a.) 微妙地

The doctor shuddered for a moment at what he saw. Then a devilish[10] look of happiness and satisfaction crept across his face.

After this day, the relationship between Roger Chillingworth and Reverend Arthur Dimmesdale changed subtly[11]. The doctor maintained his calm appearance. But secretly, he was controlling the reverend and planning to take revenge on him.

✔ *Check Up*

Why did the doctor change his attitude toward the reverend?

ⓐ He saw something on the reverend's skin.

ⓑ He felt pity for the reverend because of his illness.

ⓒ He respected the reverend's desire to keep his secret.

Ans: a

🎧 23

Dimmesdale often punished himself secretly for the crime he had committed[1]. He would force himself to go without food and sleep, and would even whip[2] himself until he was bloody. Then one night he thought of a new method[3] for self-punishment. In the middle of the night, he got dressed and quietly left the house.

As if he were walking through a dream, the reverend went to the western end of the marketplace, to the scaffolding where Hester Prynne had stood seven years earlier.

On that dark May night, the reverend climbed the steps of the scaffolding and stood on the platform atop[4] it. He felt that the town was asleep and that there was no danger of anyone discovering him.

But while he stood there, his mind was overcome with horror, and he felt the scarlet letter burning from within his breast. It was the source of his pain and illness. Then suddenly, he released a shriek[5] so long and loud that he expected the whole town to awake and come running to see him in his place of shame.

But the drowsy[6] townspeople must have thought his voice was merely the cries of wild animals or the cackles[7] of witches, because nobody came running.

1. **commit** [kə`mɪt] (v.)
   犯（罪行、過錯等）
2. **whip** [wɪp] (v.) 鞭笞；抽打
3. **method** [`mεθəd] (n.)
   （有系統的）方法
4. **atop** [ə`tɑːp] (prep.)
   在……之上

5. **shriek** [ʃriːk] (n.) 尖叫聲
6. **drowsy** [`draʊzi] (a.)
   睏的；想睡的
7. **cackle** [`kækəl] (n.)
   咯咯叫聲或笑聲

Then the reverend perceived a light approaching from the distance. When it got close enough for him to recognize the bearer[1], the reverend saw that it was Pastor Wilson. The pastor did not notice the reverend and kept walking past. The reverend knew that the pastor was coming from a late night vigil[2] in the death chamber[3] of Governor Winthrop, who had probably just passed away[4].

After the pastor passed, another light approached. This time the reverend could see that it was Hester Prynne and Pearl.

"Hester Prynne," said the reverend, "is that you?"

"Reverend Dimmesdale," exclaimed[5] Hester, who was taken by surprise[6] to find him standing atop the scaffolding in the dark. "Yes, it is Pearl and I. We are coming from Governor Winthrop's death chamber, where I measured him for a robe[7]. We're on the way back to our cottage."

---

1. **bearer** [ˋberɚr] (n.) 提物者
2. **vigil** [ˋvɪdʒɪl] (n.) 守夜
3. **death chamber**
   [dɛθ ˋtʃeɪmbɚr] (n.)
   臨終時所在的臥室
4. **pass away** 去世
5. **exclaim** [ɪkˋskleɪm] (v.)
   大叫；驚呼
6. **be taken by surprise**
   大吃一驚
7. **robe** [roʊb] (n.)
   長袍（此處特指壽衣）

"Hester, Pearl, come up here," said the reverend. "You have both been up here before, but I was not with you."

Silently, Hester held Pearl's hand, and they climbed up the steps of the platform. In the darkness, the reverend found Pearl's hand and held it. A fresh force of life poured into his heart, and the blood rushed[8] through his veins[9]. The weight was lifted[10] from his soul!

---

8. **rush** [rʌʃ] (v.) 衝；奔
9. **vein** [veɪn] (n.)
　　靜脈；〔俚〕血管

10. **lift** [lɪft] (v.) 卸除；解除

"Reverend," said little Pearl, "will you stand here tomorrow at noon with me and my mother?"

"No, not tomorrow," said the reverend. "But I shall one day."

"But when?" asked Pearl.

"I shall stand with you and your mother before the Lord on Judgment Day[1]," he answered.

1. **Judgment Day**
   [ˋdʒʌdʒmənt deɪ] (n.)
   最後審判日
2. **meteor** [ˋmiːtiər] (n.)
   流星;隕石

3. **luminescence**
   [ˌluːmɪˋnesəns] (n.) 冷光
4. **be frightened of . . .** 害怕
5. **mock** [mɑːk] (v.) 嘲弄

Pearl laughed at this, and suddenly a meteor[2] flashed and lit up the night sky. There in its luminescence[3] stood Hester with her scarlet A, the reverend, holding his hand over his heart, and Pearl, holding both their hands.

When he returned his eyes to earth, the reverend saw Pearl pointing toward a person coming closer from the distance. As the person came closer, they saw that it was Roger Chillingworth.

"Hester, who is that man?" asked the reverend. "I've become frightened of[4] him. I've started to hate him!"

"I can tell you who he is," said Pearl. Then she put her lips to the reverend's ear and whispered nonsense, and then she laughed out loud.

"Child, are you mocking[5] me?" asked the reverend.

"You are not true," said the little girl. "You won't stand here with me and mother tomorrow at noon!"

✓ *Check Up* True or False.

T F a Pearl thinks that Judgment Day will be tomorrow at noon.

T F b The reverend was delighted to see Roger coming toward them.

Ans: a. T, b. F

67

"Good sir," said Roger Chillingworth, who had come up to the scaffolding. "What ever are you doing out here at this time of night? Have you been sleepwalking[1]?"

"How did you know I was here?" asked the reverend fearfully.

"I had no idea you were here. I was just walking home from the governor's death chamber. You'd better come home with me now, or you'll not have enough energy to give your sermon tomorrow."

"Yes," said the reverend, "I'll go home with you." The man suddenly felt cold and depressed, as if rudely awaken from a dream.

After the night on the scaffolding, Hester Prynne became worried that the reverend was losing his mind[2]. She remembered her agreement[3] with Roger Chillingworth some years earlier, that she would hide his true identity as her husband.

---

1. **sleepwalk** [`sli:pwɔ:k] (v.)
   夢遊
2. **lose one's mind** 失去理智
3. **agreement** [ə`gri:mənt]
   (n.) 協議；約定
4. **intention** [ɪn`tenʃən] (n.)
   意圖；目的
5. **resolve** [rɪ`zɑ:lv] (v.)
   決定；決心
6. **tormentor** [tɔr`mɛntər]
   (n.) 施加煩惱或痛苦的人

But now she felt it was her fault for not warning the reverend of Chillingworth's terrible intentions[4]. She resolved[5] that she would speak with Chillingworth and tell him that she could no longer keep that promise. She had to tell the reverend who his tormentor[6] really was.

Hester did not have to wait long to speak with the doctor. She saw him in the forest, gathering plants one afternoon a few days later.

"Run along, and play," she said to Pearl, "I want to speak with the doctor." Then she turned to Chillingworth and said, "Doctor, I need to speak with you about an important matter."

🎧27

"Ah, Mistress[1] Hester," he said with a smile, "I hear the town council[2] may soon allow you to take that scarlet letter off your bosom."

1. **mistress** [`mɪstrɪs] (n.)
   主婦；女主人
2. **council** [`kaʊnsəl] (n.) 議會
3. **creature** [`kriːtʃər] (n.)
   生物；傢伙
4. **resemble** [rɪ`zembəl] (v.)
   相像
5. **transform** [træns`fɔːrm] (v.)
   使改變
6. **weep** [wiːp] (v.) 哭泣
   （weep-wept-wept）

"If I were worthy to be done with it, it would fall off by itself," she replied, noticing that the past seven years had transformed Chillingworth into a creature[3] that resembled[4] a devil. She knew that his life of seeking revenge must have been transforming[5] his mind, body, and soul into such a dark form.

"What do you see in my face that makes you look at it so seriously?" asked the doctor.

"Something that makes me want to weep[6]," she answered. "But let us speak of another miserable man. Seven years ago, I promised to keep your identity a secret. But I have a duty to help this man who you are slowly killing. I must tell him who you are so that he may understand why you are tormenting him."

✓ Check Up

What did Hester want to do?

a She wanted to tell the townspeople who Pearl's father was.
b She wanted to tell everyone that she was married to the doctor.
c She wanted to tell Reverend Dimmesdale who the doctor really was.

Ans: c

"That cowardly priest[1] is conscious of[2] my influence and my curse," said Chillingworth. "He's just too afraid to admit it to himself. You are foolish to want to help such a low wretch[3] as him, who abandoned[4] you with child to the mercy of this town for all these years."

"I must help him," cried Hester. "This scarlet letter instructs[5] me to do so. I will keep your secret no longer."

"Go ahead, and tell him," said Chillingworth. "I pity you for wasting your goodness on that weak shamble[6] of a man."

"I pity you, too," Hester answered. "I pity you for suffering such hatred that it has changed a wise man into a demon!"

1. **priest** [prist] (n.) 神職人員
2. **be conscious of . . .** 意識到……
3. **wretch** [rɛtʃ] (n.) 可憐的人
4. **abandon** [əˋbændən] (v.) 放棄；拋棄
5. **instruct** [ɪnˋstrʌkt] (v.) 指示
6. **shamble** [ˋʃæmbəl] (n.) 跟蹌的腳步
7. **doomed** [dumd] (a.) 命中注定的

Hester found Pearl down by the stream where she had been playing. The little girl had arranged a green A, just like her mother's, on the bosom of her dress.

"Ah, my Pearl, but your green A does not have the same meaning as the one I'm doomed[7] to wear. Do you know why I wear this letter?"

"I do," answered Pearl. "For the same reason that the reverend holds his hand over his heart."

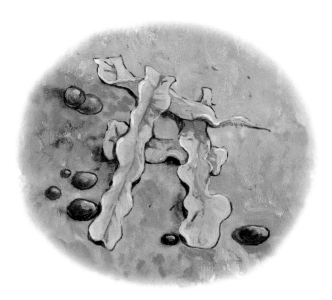

✔ *Check Up* Fill in the blank.

If you want to _____ a secret, you should tell no one about it.

Ans: keep

A True or False.

T F **1** Pearl was a very normal little girl.

T F **2** Hester Prynne wanted the town to take Pearl away from her.

T F **3** Pearl could not be forced to adapt to rules.

T F **4** Hester Prynne told Pearl they were going to the governor's mansion to return a pair of gloves the governor had asked her to embroider.

T F **5** Pearl could not accept her position as an outcast in the town.

B Select the ones that use the underlined words correctly.

1 (a) The two men soon became constant companions.

(b) He used plants from the forest to make companions.

2 (a) He pushed aside the man's hands effortlessly.

(b) The two resumed their friendship effortlessly.

3 (a) The doctor shuddered for a moment at what he saw.

(b) The shuddered leaves were ugly.

C Choose the best answer to each question.

1 Where did Pearl tell the governor and Pastor Wilson she came from?

(a) She told them she came from Heaven.

(b) She told them she came from her mother.

(c) She told them she came from the rosebush on the side of the prison.

2 Why did Chillingworth suggest they study Pearl's nature?

(a) To guess the identity of her father.

(b) Because she was so strange.

(c) To determine if she was a demon child from Hell.

3 Where did Roger Chillingworth say the ugly leaves had grown from?

(a) From the nose of the Black Man.

(b) From the heart of a man buried with a secret sin.

(c) From the rosebush growing on the side of the prison.

4 Why did Reverend Dimmesdale climb to the top of the scaffolding at night?

(a) Because he wanted to punish himself for a sin.

(b) Because he wanted to see the far side of the town.

(c) Because he wanted to enjoy a beautiful summer night.

Chapter Four

🎧 29 The Forest

Hester remained strong in her resolve to tell the reverend just who Roger Chillingworth really was. On a day Hester knew that the reverend would be passing through the forest, she set out[1] to cross his path[2], taking along little Pearl.

As they entered the forest, Pearl cried out, "Mother, the sunshine doesn't love you! It runs away and hides because of the A on your bosom!"

"Then you had better run away and try to catch it!" answered her mother. The little girl actually did catch the sun, standing amid its brilliant[3] splendor[4].

As they passed deeper into the forest, Pearl asked her mother to sit and rest for a while.

---

1. **set out** 出發；開始
2. **cross one's path**
   攔住某人的去路；
   與某人巧遇
3. **brilliant** [`brɪljənt] (a.)
   光輝的
4. **splendor** [`splɛndər] (n.)
   光輝；光彩
5. **clasp** [klæsp] (n.)
   扣環；鉤子

"Tell me a story," she demanded.

"A story about what?" asked Hester.

"A story about the Black Man who haunts the forest with his big, heavy, black book with iron clasps⁵. And tell me about how he makes people write their names in his book using their own blood! Did you ever meet the Black Man, Mother?"

One Point Lesson

Then you **had better** run away and try to catch it!
那妳最好快跑開，去設法抓住它！

had better + 原形動詞：表示「最好⋯⋯」。這個用法除了在主詞為第一人稱的句型之外，其餘都含有「勸告」、「命令」或「威嚇」的意味。

e.g. You **had better** finish your work before going to bed.
你最好先做完工作再上床睡覺。

"Who told you about this?" Hester asked.

"Last night, when we were at the house you were watching, the old woman thought I was asleep while she spoke of it. She said that the scarlet letter was the Black Man's mark on you."

"I'll tell you a story about the Black Man if you won't ask me any more afterward," said Hester. "I met the Black Man once, and this scarlet letter is his mark."

Suddenly, Hester heard footsteps[1] coming through the forest.

"Pearl, run along now, and play. I want to speak with the man who's coming toward us."

"Is it the Black Man?" inquired[2] Pearl.

"Of course not, silly child. It is the reverend."

"It is," said Pearl, who could now see the reverend coming through the darkened forest. "And he has his hand over his heart. That's because he wrote his name in the book and the Black Man put his mark over the reverend's heart. But why doesn't he wear it on the outside[3] like you?"

"Now, go, child!" cried Hester. "Stay near the stream[4], and don't go too far!"

Pearl walked away, singing to herself. Hester saw the reverend coming down the path. He looked weaker and more depressed[5] than ever.

1. **footstep** [ˋfʊtstɛp] (n.) 腳步（聲）
2. **inquire** [ɪnˋkwaɪr] (v.) 詢問
3. **on the outside** 在外部
4. **stream** [striːm] (n.) 溪流
5. **depressed** [dɪˋprɛst] (a.) 消沈的

"Arthur Dimmesdale," she called out to him. "Reverend Dimmesdale!"

"Who speaks?" answered the reverend nervously. "Hester, is that you?"

"Yes, it is I," she answered. They had not been alone together in over seven years because of their situation. They were both nervous and happy to see one another.

Fixing his eyes on her, he asked, "Hester, have you found peace?"

She smiled drearily[1] and looked down at the symbol on her bosom. "Have you?"

"No, I have found nothing but[2] darkness and despair[3]! I preach[4] purity to my followers, but I know the emptiness and agony of what I truly am. I feel like Satan is always laughing at me."

"You are wrong to torture yourself like this," said Hester. "You have repented[5] deeply for years now. You must learn to leave your sin in the past!"

"No, Hester," cried the reverend. "I'm not worthy to wear these holy garments[6] that clothe me. You are lucky to wear the A on your chest. My mark burns within me! If only I had one friend to whom I could tell the truth of my sins!"

✅ *Check Up* True or False.

[T] [F] [a] The reverend is in agony because he knows he is a hypocrite.

[T] [F] [b] Hester and Dimmesdale met together by themselves often.

Ans: a.T b.F

1. **drearily** [ˋdrɪrəli] (adv.) 沈悶地
2. **nothing but . . .** 只有……
3. **despair** [dɪˋsper] (n.) 絕望
4. **preach** [priːtʃ] (v.) 說教；傳教
5. **repent** [rɪˋpent] (v.) 後悔；懊悔
6. **garment** [ˋgɑːrmənt] (n.) 衣服（尤指外衣、外套、長袍）

"I am that friend and your partner in sin," said Hester. Then she struggled[1] to give the reverend the message that was the reason for their meeting on this day. "You also have a great enemy, who lives under the same roof as you."

"An enemy under my roof?" the reverend said with surprise. "What do you mean?"

"Oh Arthur," cried Hester. "Please forgive me. A long time ago, I agreed to deceive[2] you. The old man, the doctor whom they call Roger Chillingworth, he was my husband!"

A look of terrible violence[3] came over the reverend's face. He sank down[4] to the ground and buried his face in his hands.

"I should have known it!" groaned[5] the reverend. "My heart told me he was hiding a terrible secret from the day I first met him. Why did I not understand? Oh, Hester Prynne! You are responsible for this! I can never forgive you!" he shouted.

---

1. **struggle** [ˋstrʌgəl] (v.) 掙扎
2. **deceive** [dɪˋsiːv] (v.)
   欺騙；欺瞞
3. **violence** [ˋvaɪələns] (n.)
   激烈
4. **sink down**（膝軟地）癱倒
   （sink-sank-sunk）
5. **groan** [groun] (v.)
   呻吟；痛苦地哼聲
6. **throw one's arms around**
   伸臂環抱
   (throw-threw-thrown)
7. **over and over**
   一次又一次地

Hester Prynne threw her arms around[6] the reverend and held him close to her. His cheek rested on the scarlet letter. He tried to struggle free, but she would not let him go.

"You must forgive me," she said over and over[7]. "You must forgive me."

Check Up

Why was the reverend angry at Hester?

- a She was a married woman.
- b He blamed her for his situation.
- c She would not forgive him.

Ans: b

"Yes," cried the reverend softly. "I forgive you now. We are not the worst sinners in the world. That old man's revenge is blacker than my sin. He is killing me in cold blood. What we did was not so bad as that."

"No, what we did had a sacredness[1] of its own. We told that to each other when we made love," she whispered. "Have you forgotten?"

"No," he whispered. "I have not forgotten."

This was the gloomiest[2] hour of their lives. But in the darkness of it, there was a charm that made them linger[3] together. There they sat amid the dark forest, holding hands and kissing.

"Roger Chillingworth knows that you will reveal his identity," said the reverend. "Now he will point his finger at[4] me in front of the whole town."

1. **sacredness** ['sekrɪdnɪs] (n.) 神聖（性）
2. **gloomy** ['gluːmi] (a.) 陰暗的；晦暗的
3. **linger** ['lɪŋgər] (v.) 留連；徘徊
4. **point one's finger at** 指摘；指出
5. **passion** ['pæʃən] (n.) 慾望；激情
6. **hysterically** [hɪs'tɛrɪkli] (adv.) 歇斯底里地

"No, I don't think he'll reveal your sin to
the public," she said. "He will find other secret
ways to satisfy his dark passion[5] for revenge.
You must get away from this terrible man!"

"Yes, he's killing me," cried the reverend
hysterically[6]. "But what can I do, Hester?
Help me, please!"

One Point Lesson

What we did was **not so bad as that**.
我們犯的過錯，不及他的惡。

---

not so + adj. / adv. + as . . . : 在……方面不及……

She is **not so beautiful as** her sister.
她不如她姊姊漂亮。

"The sea brought you to this New World, and it can carry you back to the old one. You should go back to England, or you could live in Germany, France, or even in Italy."

"But how could I leave my post[1] here? Even though my soul is ruined[2], I'm needed to help others."

"You can't help anybody if you're crushed[3] under the weight of your misery[4]. You must leave this place behind," she said. "The future could be filled with new chances for success. Do anything except lay down and die!"

"Oh, Hester," cried the reverend. "I must die here. I don't have the strength or courage to risk going back into the strange, cold world alone."

1. **post** [poʊst] (n.) 崗位；職守
2. **ruined** [ˋruːɪnd] (a.) 墮落的；毀壞的
3. **crush** [krʌʃ] (v.) 壓垮；壓毀
4. **misery** [ˋmɪzəri] (n.) 不幸；痛苦
5. **unhook** [ʌnˋhʊk] (v.) 把鈎鬆開
6. **glitter** [ˋglɪtər] (v.) 閃閃發光

Then in a deep whisper, Hester replied,
"You will not go alone."

At this, Arthur Dimmesdale looked into her
eyes with joy and hope.

"We won't look back," said Hester. "The past
is gone. See!"

Then with her fingers she unhooked[5] the
scarlet letter from her breast and flung it away
from her onto a rock at the edge of the
stream. The letter lay there, glittering[6] like a
lost jewel.

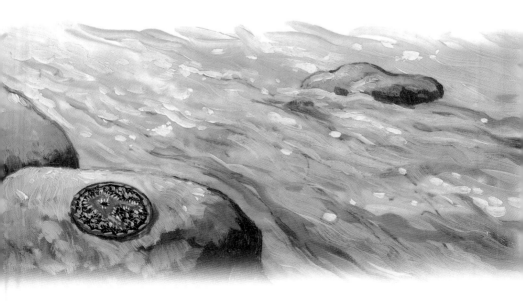

Hester heaved[1] a huge sigh of relief[2] as the burden of shame and anguish[3] left her heart. The freedom she felt made her realize what a weight it had truly been. Hester undid[4] her cap and let her dark, beautiful hair fall down around her shoulders. Then the sunlight came through the tops of the trees and flooded the forest.

Hester looked again at the reverend with eyes full of joy and said, "Now you must get to know our little Pearl! You have seen her, but you do not really know her yet! She's a strange child, but you will learn to love her dearly[5]."

"Do you think she will want to know me?" asked the reverend hopefully, "I have always been afraid of little Pearl."

"Ah, that is so sad," answered Hester. "She will love you dearly. She is not far off now. I will call her. Pearl! Pearl!"

1. **heave** [hi:v] (v.) 費力地發出嘆息
2. **relief** [rɪ`li:f] (n.) 緩和；解除
3. **anguish** [`æŋgwɪʃ] (n.) 極度的痛苦
4. **undo** [ʌn`du:] (v.) 解開（undo-undid-undone）
5. **dearly** [`dɪrli] (adv.) 由衷地
6. **obey** [ou`beɪ] (v.) 服從
7. **devoid** [dɪ`vɔɪd] (a.) 缺乏的
8. **stamp** [stæmp] (v.) 踩（腳）

Pearl was away, gathering up flowers for her mother. She heard the call and came back toward them slowly.

"Come here," said Hester. "I want you to become a dear friend of the reverend."

But Pearl did not obey[6] her mother's command. The child only pointed to her mother's breast, devoid[7] of the scarlet letter, and stamped[8] her foot.

✓ *Check Up* True or False.

T F [a] Hester regretted throwing the scarlet letter away.

T F [b] Hester wanted Dimmesdale to teach Pearl how to behave herself.

Ans: a. F b. F

"I see," said Hester. "Small children don't like to see the things they've always known change even slightly[1]. She is missing the letter that she's seen on me since the day she was born." Hester pointed to the letter at the edge of the stream and said, "There's the letter, Pearl. Bring it to me now."

"You pick it up yourself," replied Pearl.

Frustrated[2] with the child, Hester sighed and walked to the side of the stream and hooked[3] the letter back on her breast.

"Do you know your mother now, child?" she said to her daughter.

"Yes, now you are my mother indeed!" said little Pearl, bounding[4] across the stream to join them.

"Come and see him, Pearl. He wants to greet you. He loves you. Will you love him, too?" asked Hester.

1. **slightly** [`slaɪtli] (adv.) 稍微地
2. **frustrated** [`frʌstreɪtɪd] (a.) 感到挫折的
3. **hook** [hʊk] (v.) 以鉤子扣
4. **bound** [baʊnd] (v.) 跳躍
5. **hand in hand** 手牽手
6. **stoop** [stuːp] (v.) 屈身；彎腰
7. **apart from . . .** 與……相隔

"Does he really love us?" Pearl asked, looking at her mother in the eyes with sharp intelligence. "Will he walk hand in hand[5] with us into town?"

"Not now, child," answered Hester. "But soon he will be with us all the time."

"And will he always keep his hand over his heart?" Pearl inquired.

Dimmesdale, embarrassed by the child's questions, stooped[6] over and kissed her forehead, hoping to soften her view of him.

But as soon as his lips left her forehead, she ran to the stream and washed the kiss off her brow, as if it were something dirty. Then she stayed apart from[7] her mother and the reverend while they discussed their plans to be together in the near future.

✓ *Check Up*

Which is the best word to describe Pearl?

  a Spoiled   b Dutiful   c Respectful

Ans: a

The Symbols in the *Scarlet Letter*

Hawthorne used symbols throughout the *Scarlet Letter* to reinforce[1] his main ideas. The most important symbol in the *Scarlet Letter* is, of course, the red letter "A" itself. This letter stands for[2] "adultery" and is an obvious[3] symbol of Hester's sin.

However, Hester wears it proudly, and it changes meanings as time passes. Eventually, it can be seen as a symbol for "able". Pearl, Hester's daughter, serves as a symbol of a living version of the scarlet letter. She is troublesome, and this punishes Hester. On the other hand, she is also a blessing. Pearl gives her mother reason to live.

Compared to Pearl, the scarlet letter is almost useless because Pearl is a symbol of the passion that created the sin. This reflects the uselessness of the Puritan "punishment" that is given to Hester. Hester would not give in[4] to their demands, and instead becomes a proud and independent woman.

Another symbol appears in the form of the meteor that lights up the night sky as Dimmesdale stands on the scaffolding with Hester and Pearl. Just after he tells Pearl he will stand with her mother on Judgment Day, this light from this meteor "reveals" to the world that Dimmesdale belongs with Hester and Pearl. We find out later that he is actually Pearl's father.

These types of symbols are literary[5] techniques that authors use to help reinforce their main themes.

1. **reinforce** [ˌriːɪnˈfɔːrs] (v.) 強調
2. **stand for** 代表；意味
3. **obvious** [ˈɑːbvɪəs] (a.) 顯而易見的
4. **give in** 屈服；讓步
5. **literary** [ˈlɪtəreri] (a.) 文學的

Chapter Five

🎧 37 The Revelation[1]

After leaving the forest, the reverend could not believe their meeting had been real. They had decided that the cities of Europe would be the best place for them to begin their new lives. And it happened that there was a ship in Boston Harbor[2] set to leave for the Old World in four days. Through Hester's charity work, she knew the ship's captain and was able to make arrangements that she, the reverend, and Pearl would depart[3] with the ship.

When Hester told the reverend of her arrangement, he was overjoyed[4] and remarked, "How fortunate, as I'm set to give the election[5] sermon in only three days' time."

---

1. **revelation** [ˌrevəˈleɪʃən] (n.) 天啟；揭露
2. **harbor** [ˈhɑːrbər] (n.) 港口
3. **depart** [dɪˈpɑːrt] (v.) 啟程
4. **overjoyed** [ˌouvərˈdʒɔɪd] (a.) 狂喜的
5. **election** [ɪˈlekʃən] (n.) 選舉
6. **commemorate** [kəˈmeməreɪt] (v.) 紀念；祝賀
7. **swearing-in** [ˈswɛrɪŋ ɪn] (n.) 使當選人或證人等宣誓
8. **high point** 顛峰
9. **possess** [pəˈzes] (v.) 擁有

The election sermon, to commemorate[6] the swearing-in[7] of the new governor, was the high point[8] in the career of any New England clergyman.

Dimmesdale returned from his talk with Hester possessing[9] a sense of great physical energy that was very unusual for him. He found that no matter what he did, he could not become tired.

One Point Lesson

He found that **no matter what** he did, he could not become tired.
他發覺無論做什麼事，他都不會覺得累。

---

no matter what：無論如何（= whatever）

e.g. **No matter what** I say, he will not believe me.
無論我說什麼，他都不會相信我。

🎧 38

Finally, the reverend entered the peace and solitude[1] of his study, where he could write his most important election sermon. While he was occupied with[2] this task, there came a knock on the door.

When the reverend said, "Come in," he feared he would behold[3] an evil spirit, and he did. It was Roger Chillingworth. The reverend remained speechless.

1. **solitude** [`sɑːlɪtuːd] (n.)
   獨處；幽靜處

2. **be occupied with . . .**
   埋首於……

3. **behold** [bɪ`hoʊld] (v.)
   看見（不尋常之人事物）

4. **assistance** [ə`sɪstəns] (n.)
   協助；幫助

5. **solemnly** [`sɑːləmli] (adv.)
   莊重地；正經地

6. **renewal** [rɪ`nuːəl] (n.)
   復原；恢復

7. **Heaven grant it . . .**
   求上帝賜允……

8. **frame** [freɪm] (n.)
   體格；框架

"Hello, Reverend," said Chillingworth. "I suspect you will need my medical assistance[4] to help you put your heart and strength into the task of making the election sermon."

"Not this time," answered the reverend solemnly[5]. "My recent walk through the woods has provided me with a renewal[6] of spirit and energy. I will not need any of your drugs."

They both knew that they were no longer trusted friends, but rather bitter enemies.

"Reverend, are you sure you shouldn't use my services to help you make this most important sermon? Heaven knows you may not be here next year to make another one."

"Yes, Heaven grant it[7], I'll be in a better world," replied the reverend. "But in my present frame[8] of body, I don't need your medicine."

"Well, I'm glad to hear it," said the doctor.

✓ Check Up

Why did the doctor come to see the reverend?
a He wanted to help the reverend write his speech.
b He wanted to bid the reverend farewell.
c He wanted to give the reverend some medicine.

Ans: c

39

After the doctor left, the reverend called his servant to bring him a large meal. He devoured[1] the food like an animal that had not eaten for a long time. Then he spent all night flinging written pages of his sermon from the desk, as if Heaven was transmitting[2] the words through his hand.

When the reverend awoke in the morning, the pen was still between his fingers, and the sermon was marvelously completed.

On the day of the new governor's inauguration[3], the marketplace was crowded with the townspeople, who were waiting to see the procession[4] of officials pass and to hear the reverend's sermon. Hester and Pearl joined the crowd.

Everywhere around them were festivities[5], wrestling[6] matches[7], and contests[8]. The strict Puritan society was filled with people who were as joyful as they were allowed to be.

---

1. **devour** [dɪˋvaʊr] (v.) 狼吞虎嚥地吃
2. **transmit** [trænsˋmɪt] (v.) 傳達
3. **inauguration** [ɪˌnɔgjəˋreʃən] (n.) 就職；就職典禮
4. **procession** [prəˋseʃən] (n.) 隊伍；行列

5. **festivity** [feˋstɪvɪti] (n.) 慶祝活動
6. **wrestling** [ˋresəlɪŋ] (n.) 摔角的
7. **match** [mætʃ] (n.) 比賽
8. **contest** [ˋkɑːntest] (n.) 比賽
9. **spot** [spɑːt] (v.) 發現；認出

When Pearl asked if the reverend would be there, Hester said, "Yes, but he won't be joining us. And we shouldn't speak to him if we see him today."

Roger Chillingworth also came to the festival. When Hester first spotted[9] him, he was speaking with the captain of the ship that would be leaving for Europe on the following day.

40

When Hester later spoke to the captain, he told her that Chillingworth would be joining them on the voyage[1]. Her heart sank at the fearful news, and when she saw Chillingworth, she felt his smile hid a terrible, secret meaning. But Hester had no time to think about the captain's shocking news.

The time was at hand[2] for the reverend to give his sermon. When she saw the Reverend Dimmesdale, she felt as though he were another person whom she had never seen before. She felt sad, as if he were in another world.

Then Hester saw Mistress Hibbins, who asked her if she had met the reverend in the forest recently. Hester denied it. But Mistress Hibbins continued to tell her that the reverend had been there and signed his name in the Black Man's book. She said the Black Man had his way of leaving a mark on those who would not admit they had signed his book.

---

1. **voyage** [ˋvɔɪdʒ] (n.)
   航行；航海
2. **at hand**
   即將到來的；在手邊的
3. **outlying** [ˋaʊtˌlaɪɪŋ] (a.)
   外圍的；偏遠的
4. **encircle** [ɪnˋsɜːrkəl] (v.)
   包圍；團團圍住

To make matters worse for Hester Prynne, the festival had brought to town many people from outlying[3] areas. These people encircled[4] her, staring and pointing at her mark of shame.

Check Up

What terrible news did the ship's captain tell Hester?
- a That the doctor would also be sailing on the ship
- b That the ship would be delayed for several months
- c That the reverend would not be leaving with them

Ans: a

On this day, Hester felt more pain than she had on the first day she had worn the letter. What nobody knew was that the same mark of disgrace¹ burned on the saintly² Reverend Dimmesdale.

1. **disgrace** [dɪs`greɪs] (n.)
   不名譽；恥辱
2. **saintly** [`seɪntli] (a.)
   聖人般的

3. **eloquent** [`eləkwənt] (a.)
   有說服力的
4. **pedestal** [`pedɪstəl] (n.)
   台；座

It was at this time that the reverend's powerful and eloquent[3] voice could be heard throughout the marketplace, coming from a high pedestal[4] at the eastern end of the marketplace. People were brought to silence by his profound[5] words. Many people said that never before had they heard so wise, so high, and so holy a spirit speak as they heard on that day.

Through his powerful waves of Heaven-inspired[6] words, the reverend reached his proudest peak[7] of glory, as he stood atop the pedestal.

Meanwhile, Hester and Pearl stood next to the old scaffolding with the symbol still burning on her breast.

5. **profound** [prə`faʊnd] (a.)
   深刻的

6. **inspire** [ɪn`spaɪr] (v.)
   給予靈感

7. **peak** [piːk] (n.) 顛峰；山頂

 Check Up

Which of the following three descriptions is wrong?

- a Hester's most shameful day was also the reverend's greatest.
- b Many newcomers made Hester feel ashamed.
- c The reverend delivered Heaven's profound words.

Ans: b

When the reverend's sermon was finished, music began, and a procession of honorable town fathers began walking on a pathway[1] through the crowds of people.

When they reached the western end of the marketplace, the people cheered. As the shouts died down, Hester saw the reverend, and was shocked at how very pale and weak he looked. It was as if he had used the last of his energy to deliver[2] his powerful and grand[3] sermon.

Now he appeared to be a feeble[4] man who could barely[5] stand by himself. Pastor Wilson hurried to the reverend's side and tried to hold his arm for fear that he would fall, but the reverend shook him off. He kept walking on his own, like a shaky[6] infant. By this time, he was very near the old scaffold.

The crowd looked at him in shock, wondering if his earthly faintness[7] was just another sign of his heavenly strength. Suddenly, the reverend turned toward the scaffold and held out[8] his arms.

---

1. **pathway** [ˈpæθweɪ] (n.) 路；小徑
2. **deliver** [dɪˈlɪvər] (v.) 發表；宣講
3. **grand** [grænd] (a.) 崇高的
4. **feeble** [ˈfiːbl̩] (a.) 虛弱的
5. **barely** [ˈberli] (adv.) 勉強地
6. **shaky** [ˈʃeɪki] (a.) 搖晃的

"Hester," he cried, "my little Pearl, come here to me!" The look on his face was one of terrible pain. But Pearl ran to him and threw her arms around him. Hester, as if forced by invisible[9] hands, slowly approached him.

7. **faintness** [ˋfeɪntnɪs] (n.)
   虛弱
8. **hold out** 伸出

9. **invisible** [ɪnˋvɪzɪbəl] (a.)
   看不見的

Together, with Hester supporting the reverend's weight and Pearl holding his hand, they climbed up the steps of the scaffolding together.

The Scarlet Letter

"Are you mad?" whispered Roger Chillingworth, who stood near them. "Stand away from that woman and child! You will blacken[1] your good name and be cast[2] into the pit[3] of dishonor! I can't help you after this!"

"Ha ha," the reverend laughed at Chillingworth. "Tempter[4], you are too late this time. With God's help, I will escape you now!"

The crowd watched in an uproar[5] as the three stood on the scaffolding. The noble men of rank[6] and dignity could not understand the meaning of his actions.

Old Chillingworth followed them, as if he were just another actor in their guilty drama, on stage for the final act[7]. Looking darkly at the reverend, he said, "You could have searched the Earth for a place to hide from me. There is no place high or low where you could have escaped to, except for this very scaffolding."

1. **blacken** [ˋblækən] (v.)
   弄黑；玷污
2. **cast** [kæst] (v.) 投；擲
   （cast-cast-cast）
3. **pit** [pɪt] (n.) 坑；洞

4. **tempter** [ˋtɛmptər] (n.)
   誘惑者（字首大寫時專指
   撒旦）
5. **uproar** [ˋʌprɔːr] (n.) 騷動
6. **rank** [ræŋk] (n.) 階級；地位
7. **act** [ækt] (n.)（一）幕

44

The reverend looked to Hester, "Isn't this better than the plans we made in the forest?"

"I don't know. It may lead to the death of us all," she replied.

"God will protect you and Pearl. As for me, I am a dying man. This is my last chance to accept the truth of my shame."

Then, the reverend faced the other clergymen, the governor, the noblemen, and the crowd of townspeople.

"People of New England!" he cried in a solemn and majestic[1] voice. "Behold me, a shameful sinner! I should have stood here seven years ago when the governor demanded to know the name of Hester Prynne's partner in sin! You have all seen the scarlet letter that this woman wears. But there has stood one among you whose brand of shame and infamy[2] you have not seen!"

---

1. **majestic** [mə`dʒɛstɪk] (a.)
   莊嚴的；威嚴的
2. **infamy** [`ɪnfəmi] (n.)
   不名譽；惡名
3. **collapse** [kə`læps] (v.)
   倒塌；倒下
4. **manage to** 設法；勉力
5. **witness** [`wɪtnɪs] (v.)
   目擊；親睹

At this point, the reverend's weakness was so great that he nearly collapsed[3]. But he managed to[4] stand by himself and stepped forward, away from Hester and Pearl. "But now you must witness[5] the great power of the Lord and the true mark of shame. Behold!"

| One Point Lesson |

At this point, the reverend's weakness was **so great that** he nearly collapsed.
說到這兒，牧師虛弱得差一點倒下。

---

so + adj. + that . . .：如此地……，以致於……

e.g. She was **so happy that** she couldn't say a word.
她快樂到一個字都說不出來。

45

With a quick motion[1], the reverend tore away[2] his holy robe to expose his bare chest. The crowd was horror-stricken[3] as they gazed upon the terrible miracle emblazoned[4] upon the flesh of his breast. The reverend had a look of victory on his face shortly before he collapsed to the floor of the scaffold.

Hester raised his head in her hands, and old Chillingworth knelt down by him and said, "You have escaped me! You have escaped me!"

"My little Pearl," the reverend said to the child beside him. "Will you kiss me now?"

The girl leaned forward and kissed his lips. And with her kiss, the spell[5] of grief[6] that had been over her all her life was broken. Her tears fell on her father's cheek.

"Farewell, Hester," said the reverend.

---

1. **motion** [ˈmouʃən] (n.) 動作
2. **tear away** 扯開
   （tear-tore-torn）
3. **horror-stricken** (a.)
   [ˈhɔːrər ˈstrɪkən] 受驚嚇的
4. **emblazon** [ɪmˈbleɪzən] (v.)
   用紋章裝飾
5. **spell** [spɛl] (n.) 魔咒
6. **grief** [griːf] (n.) 悲傷；悲痛
7. **awe** [ɔː] (n.) 敬畏；畏懼

"Shall we not meet again in Heaven? Shall we not spend our eternal lives together? Certainly we've paid enough of a price for that," she said to him.

"Only merciful God knows," said the reverend. "If He had not brought me here to tell the truth to these people, I would have been lost forever. Praise to His name! His will is done! Farewell!"

With that word came the reverend's last breath. The crowd was silently still, in a state of shock and awe[7].

✓ *Check Up*

How did the doctor feel about the reverend's actions?

a He felt elated.

b He felt disappointed.

c He felt victorious.

46

As the days passed, many people spoke of the scarlet letter, just like Hester's, that they had seen imprinted[1] on the reverend's breast.

Some thought he had inflicted[2] it upon himself through terrible self-torture. Others thought that Roger Chillingworth had used drugs and magic spells to inflict it upon him. And still others believed that Heaven had placed it there to punish him for his sin.

1. **imprint** [`ɪmprɪnt] (v.) 印記
2. **inflict** [ɪn`flɪkt] (v.) 加諸
3. **authority** [ə`θɔrəti] (n.) 當局；官方
4. **defend** [dɪ`fend] (v.) 辯護
5. **character** [`kærɪktər] (n.) 人格；品行
6. **declare** [dɪ`kler] (v.) 聲稱；宣稱
7. **moral** [`mɔːrəl] (n.) 寓意；道德上的教訓
8. **stand out** 突出；顯目
9. **ultimately** [`ʌltəmətli] (adv.) 最終地；終極地

Many of the religious authorities[3] defended[4] Reverend Dimmesdale's character[5] and pronounced that his dying words declared[6] no guilt in the matter of Hester Prynne and her daughter.

They said that the reverend had merely used his last Earthly moments to deliver a powerful sermon through his own example. But the moral[7] that stood out[8] from the poor reverend's miserable experience was ultimately[9], "Be true! Be true! Be true!"

47

After the object of Roger Chillingworth's quest[1] for revenge was gone, the old man simply withered[2] away into nothing. He died within the same year and left a great amount of money and property[3] to Hester Prynne's little daughter Pearl.

Pearl and Hester disappeared for some time after that. But eventually[4], Pearl became the richest heiress[5] in the New World, and Hester Prynne returned to her little cottage to continue her simple existence[6] of hard work and charity.

1. **quest** [kwest] (n.) 探索
2. **wither** [ˋwɪðər] (v.) 凋零；枯萎
3. **property** [ˋprɑːpərti] (n.) 財產
4. **eventually** [ɪˋventʃuəli] (adv.) 結果；終於
5. **heiress** [ˋeəres] (n.) 女繼承人
6. **existence** [ɪgˋzɪstəns] (n.) 存在；生存
7. **tombstone** [ˋtuːmstoʊn] (n.) 墓碑
8. **shield** [ʃiːld] (n.) 盾；盾形（物）
9. **engrave** [ɪnˋgreɪv] (v.) 雕刻
10. **inscription** [ɪnˋskrɪpʃən] (n.) 銘文；銘刻

When she finally died at a very old age, she was buried next to an unmarked grave, which along with hers shared a single blank tombstone[7]. Some years later, there mysteriously appeared a shield[8] engraved[9] on the tombstone. If one were to read it, they would see the inscription[10], "On a Black Background, the Letter A in Red."

✔ *Check Up* True or False.

T F (a) Hester and Pearl lived out their lives in luxury.

T F (b) After Dimmesdale died, Roger seemed to have nothing to live for.

Ans: a. F b. T

A Fill in the blanks with the given words.

> devoured   frame   occupied   crowd

❶ While he was _____ with the task, there came a knock on the door.

❷ But in my present _____ of body, I don't need your medicine.

❸ He _____ the food as if he were an animal that had not eaten for a long time.

❹ Hester and Pearl joined the _____.

B True or false.

T F ❶ Hester Prynne never told Dimmesdale that Chillingworth was her husband.

T F ❷ Pearl was happy when Dimmesdale kissed her.

T F ❸ Reverend Dimmesdale and Hester held hands and kissed in the forest.

T F ❹ Hester told Reverend Dimmesdale that she and Pearl would go away with him.

C Choose the right answer to each question.

❶ What did Hester do after she and Reverend Dimmesdale agreed to run away together?

(a) She gave him a big kiss on the lips.

(b) She slapped his face.

(c) She took the scarlet letter off her breast.

❷ What happened when Pearl kissed Reverend Dimmesdale's lips on the scaffolding?

(a) She was arrested.

(b) The spell of grief over her life was broken.

(c) She had to wear a scarlet A.

D Rearrange the sentences in chronological order.

❶ Reverend Dimmesdale became angry that Hester hadn't told him Chillingworth was her husband.

❷ Reverend Dimmesdale and Hester Prynne decided to leave the colony.

❸ People encircled Hester Prynne, staring and pointing at the mark on her bosom.

❹ Reverend Dimmesdale wrote his election sermon enthusiastically.

❺ Hester Prynne begged Dimmesdale to forgive her.

_____ ⇨ _____ ⇨ _____ ⇨ _____ ⇨ _____

Appendixes

1. Guide to Listening Comprehension
2. Listening Guide
3. Listening Comprehension

Guide to Listening Comprehension

 When listening to the story, use some of the techniques shown below. If you take time to study some phonetic characteristics of English, listening will be easier.

Get in the flow of English.

English creates a rhythm formed by combinations of strong and weak stress intonations. Each word has its particular stress that combines with other words to form the overall pattern of stress or rhythm in a particular sentence.

When you are speaking and listening to English, it is essential to get in the flow of the rhythm of English. It takes a lot of practice to get used to such a rhythm. So, you need to start by identifying the stressed syllable in a word.

Listen for the strongly stressed words and phrases.

In English, key words and phrases that are essential to the meaning of a sentence are stressed louder. Therefore, pay attention to the words stressed with a higher pitch. When listening to an English recording for the first time, what matters most is to listen for a general understanding of what you hear. Do not try to hear every single word. Most of the unstressed words are articles or auxiliary verbs, which don't play an important role in the general context. At this level, you can ignore them.

Pay attention to liaisons.

In reading English, words are written with a space between them. There isn't such an obvious guide when it comes to listening to English. In oral English, there are many cases when the sounds of words are linked with adjacent words.

For instance, let's think about the phrase "**take off**," which can be used in "take off your clothes." "Take off your clothes" doesn't sound like [teɪk ɔːf] with each of the words completely and clearly separated from the others. Instead, it sounds as if almost all the words in context are slurred together, [ˈteɪkɔːf], for a more natural sound.

Shadow the voice of the native speaker.

Finally, you need to mimic the voice of the native speaker. Once you are sure you know how to pronounce all the words in a sentence, try to repeat them like an echo. Listen to the book again, but this time you should try a fun exercise while listening to the English.

This exercise is called "shadowing." The word "shadow" means a dark shade that is formed on a surface. When used as a verb, the word refers to the action of following someone or something like a shadow. In this exercise, pretend you are a parrot and try to shadow the voice of the native speaker.

Try to mimic the reader's voice by speaking at the same speed, with the same strong and weak stresses on words, and pausing or stopping at the same points.

Experts have already proven this technique to be effective. If you practice this shadowing exercise, your English speaking and listening skills will improve by leaps and bounds. While shadowing the native speaker, don't forget to pay attention to the meaning of each phrase and sentence.

Step 1 Listen to what you want to shadow many times. Start out by just trying to shadow a few words or a sentence.

Step 2 Mimic the CD out loud. You can shadow everything the speaker says as if you are singing a round, or you also can speak simultaneously with the recorded voice of the native speaker.

Step 3 As you practice more, try to shadow more. For instance, shadow a whole sentence or paragraph instead of just a few words.

Chapter One pages 14–15

Although the (❶) ( ) the Boston Colony strove to create a utopian society, two of the first things they built when they made their town were a cemetery and a prison. On this day, twenty years after the (❷) ( ) settlers arrived in the New World colony, the townspeople gathered outside the prison.

"Good women," proclaimed one woman, "If we judged wicked women like Hester Prynne, she (❸) not have the easy sentence that the town magistrates have handed her!"

"Yes!" agreed (❹) ( ). "They should at least brand the mark upon her forehead with a hot iron! By placing the mark on the front of her gown, she can cover it up anytime!"

"Yes!" cried another, "She may cover it as she likes, but the mark will always be on her heart!"

Then the prison door, covered in iron spikes, flew open. A large, (❺) figure in black came out from the inner darkness.

一開始若能聽清楚發音，之後就沒有聽力的負擔。首先，請聽過摘錄的章節，之後再反覆聆聽括弧內單字的發音，並仔細閱讀各種發音的說明。

以下都是以英語的典型發音為基礎，所做的簡易說明，即使這裡未提到的發音，也可以配合音檔反覆聆聽，如此一來聽力必能更上層樓。

❶ **forefathers of:** 美式英文在發音時，若前一個字有三個音節以上，而後續的字只有一個音節，那後方單音節的字便會輕讀。在這個例子裡，forefathers 的字尾 s 讀起來與 of 會連在一起，甚至包括接下去的 the，讀音也幾乎聽不出來。此外，forefathers 的重音在第一音節 fore，所以 fathers 輕讀就可以了。

❷ **first Puritan:** 當 st 是在字尾連在一起時，因為兩個字母都是吐氣音，故而讀音多半只聽得出 s。如果前一個字的字尾是子音，且接下來的字的字首也是子音，那為了清楚讀出子音字首，前一個字的子音字尾就會含糊帶過。如此例，st 接 p，讀音會聽起來像 firs Puritan。

❸ **would:** would、should、could，這三個字的 oul 輕讀時都發 [ə]，重讀時才發 [ʊ]。一般而言，除非是要強調這幾個字，否則都是輕讀。否定句的重音會放在 not，所以這三個字必定輕讀，同時因為 not 字首是子音 n，故而前字的字尾 d 幾乎聽不出來。

❹ **another woman:** another 這個字重音在 o，且注意 a 發音為 [ə]，因此與 er 一樣讀音很輕。woman 這個字，要注意 o 的發音為短母音 [ʊ]，不是 [ɔ] 或長母音 [o]。

❺ **frightening:** 這個字要注意 en 的 e 不發音。ten 的發音是 [tn]，讀音時 t 含在口裡，不把氣音吐出，而與 n 合在一起。這樣的發音例子不少，如 cotton、gotten、bitten，但是一般往往因為 [tn] 發音不容易，或以為 e 要發音，而把它讀成 [tən]。

With his hand, he (**1**) (   ) usher out a young woman. But she pushed the hand away and stepped out into the open by her own free will, with an air of dignity.

In the woman's arms was a three-month-old baby. The baby winked because it was the first time it had ever (**2**) (   ) on its face. The mother, standing fully revealed amid the townspeople, lowered the baby in her arm to (**3**) (   ) (   ). She was blushing, but she wore a proud smile. On the breast of her gown was a large (**4**) A. The letter was made of fine, red cloth and embroidered with rich, gold thread. The design was artistic and fanciful.

Hester Prynne was a tall young woman, with an elegant figure and dark gleaming hair. Those who knew her were amazed at her beauty and ladylike comportment under these circumstances.

"She certainly has (**5**) (   ) with the sewing needle," remarked one of the women, "but what a shameful way to show it!"

"Make way in the King's name!" shouted the prison officer. "Everyone will have a chance to (**6**)(   ) good view of this wicked woman from now until noon. Come along, Hester. Show your scarlet letter in the marketplace!"

❶ tried to: 因為 to 的字首 t 與 tried 的字尾 d 發音相近，故兩個字連在一起時，d 要退居幕後，含在口中，所以聽起來會像是 trie to [traɪ tʊ]。

❷ felt sunlight: felt 的字尾是 t，sunlight 的字首是 s，當 t 與 s 連在一起，t 的讀音會近似 [d]。其他相似規則還有 p 跟 k，當氣音 p、k 與 s 相連時，無論 s 是在前或在後，p 與 k 的讀音會近似 [b] 與 [g]。此外，felt 的 [l] 發音是要把舌頭上翹，停在接近上牙齦內側處。

❸ show her gown: her 這個字，由於字首為無聲 h，故當前一字的字尾是母音時，h 就需要發音；當前一字的字尾是子音時，h 則常不用發音。例如跟在 have 或 had 的後面時，he、him、her 的 h 就不用唸出來。

❹ letter: 美式英文中，無論 letter 前後連接什麼字，都要輕巧地讀。letter 雖然是 double t，但只發一個 t，而 t 是吐氣音。

❺ great skill: 這兩個字相連時，讀音與 ❷ 相同。也就是，當前一字的字尾是 t，而接續字的字首是 s 時，t 的讀音近似 d，要含在口裡。而 skill 這個字，因為 k 是接在 s 的後面，讀音要變成 g。

❻ get a: 這兩個字連在一起時，a 的讀音要輕，發音為 [ə]。

🎧 50 **A** Listen to the MP3 and write down the sentences, then match the characters described.

a Hester Prynne   **b** Roger Chillingworth   **c** Dimmesdale   **d** Pearl

1 _____ _____

2 _____ _____

3 _____ _____

4 _____ _____

🎧 51 **B** Listen to the MP3 and fill in the blanks.

1 The _____ of Boston Colony strove to create a _____ society.

2 She was _____ to be in the _____ of the crowd.

3 When Hester refused, Pearl _____ into a fit of tears and an ear-piercing _____.

4 She smiled _____ and looked down at the symbol on her _____.

5 The reverend _____ _____.

52 **C** Write down the questions that may be answered by the following sentences.

1 _____?

    (a) He was traveling around the world.

    (b) He was in medical school.

    (c) He was being held prisoner by the heathen savages.

2 _____?

    (a) He got it done at a tattoo parlor.

    (b) He inscribed it on himself as self-punishment

    (c) Hester Prynne carved the A into his chest.

53 **D** True or False.

T F **1**
....

T F **2**
....

T F **3**
....

T F **4**
....

T F **5**
....

霍桑（Nathaniel Hawthorne, 1804–1864）

　　霍桑是位美國小說家與短篇故事作家，出生在嚴格的清教家庭，自幼喜好閱讀。大學畢業後，他開始為家鄉的雜誌撰寫故事。1837 年，第一本小說出世，使他以嚴肅的作家形象為人所知。《紅字》（*The Scarlet Letter*）則出版於 1850 年。

　　霍桑以描寫人性罪惡與心理問題著名。在作品中，他細膩地探究何為罪惡與人類良知。由於自身的成長背景，霍桑尤其對清教傳統感興趣，他好奇宗教理念如何反應在恪守信條的信眾上，他們的內在聲音、道德、宗教信仰與行為表現，又是如何與信仰互動。霍桑寫出了那些因信仰而苦於罪惡感的人，以及沈溺孤獨的人。

　　《紅字》是霍桑最著名的作品，其他名作還有《古宅青苔》（*Mosses from an Old Manse*, 1846）、《七角樓》（*The House with Seven Gables*, 1851）、《福谷傳奇》（*The Blithedale Romance*, 1852）、《纏繞樹林的故事》（*Tanglewood Tales*, 1853）與《玉石雕像》（*The Marble Faun*, 1860）。

　　《紅字》描述一段環繞賀絲特・普林、狄默斯岱爾牧師與羅傑・齊林沃斯的三角戀情。故事背景在 17 世紀中期，時為殖民地的波士頓裡，一段偷情帶來的種種後果。書中細細描繪出在嚴苛的清教社會裡，主角飽受傳統道德經年累月的俗規折磨，引發內心的悲傷、孤獨與後悔。

　　賀絲特・普林獨居於波士頓，丈夫據說在海上失蹤了。賀絲特懷孕產下一名女嬰，取名珍珠，卻因此受大眾污名指責，被迫在衣服繡上紅色字母「Ａ」，如此一來，每個遇見她的人都知道她犯下了偷情（adultery）的罪。雖然賀絲特拒絕向外透露，但其實她的情人，正是年輕神聖的地方牧師：亞瑟・狄默斯岱爾。

　　賀絲特的丈夫羅傑・齊林沃斯在外多時，當賀絲特在城裡受公眾懲處時，他卻再次現身。但羅傑沒有揭開自己的真實身分。他決心找出賀絲特的情人，並向他展開報復。

　　年輕的亞瑟・狄默斯岱爾牧師由於偷情，受到強烈罪惡感的譴責，心力交瘁的他，最後在賀絲特的懷中告解，並沒了呼吸。故事結尾，賀絲特決定帶著女兒珍珠前往歐洲，開始新的人生。

p. 12–13

Hester Prynne 賀絲特・普林

我是一個外表美麗、個性獨立,卻命運乖舛的女子。我已婚,但和別的男人發生關係,並且生下了一女。現在市民要我抖出孩子的父親究竟是誰!但我是不會講的,我決不可能去背叛另一個人。

Reverend Dimmesdale 狄默斯岱爾牧師

啊,我是活得這麼的卑鄙!我告訴人們,要行為端正,按上帝的旨意行事。雖然我還很年輕,但是人們很尊重我。然而,我並不值得他們尊敬,我有一個可怕祕密,在我心上燒得灼痛。喔,我該如何洗去罪惡、重獲自由呀?

Pearl 珍珠

別的小孩都有父親,我卻沒有!不過,我並不會為此過於苦惱。我大部分的時間,都可以隨心所欲地玩耍,或是為所欲為。大人們覺得我很不懂規矩,但他們都正經八百的,讓我覺得很無趣!

Roger Chillingworth 羅傑・齊林沃斯

我的妻子趁我不在時,和別的男人有了孩子。但我不怪她,她總是對我說,她並不愛我。不過,我認為孩子的生父的確有錯。我會把那個男人揪出來。他不敢吭聲真是懦弱,我會為此好好修理他。

Pastor John Wilson & Governor Bellingham
約翰・威爾森牧師 & 貝林漢市長

我們的職責，是確保清教徒社會確實遵循著上帝的旨意。賀絲特・普林必須告訴我們，她孩子的父親究竟是誰，否則就無法獲得上帝的寬恕。

［第一章］可怕的罪

p. 14–15　儘管波士頓殖民地的祖先們當年竭力要創建一個烏托邦式的社會，但他們在建城時，最先搭造的兩座建築物，卻是墓園和監獄。這一天，市民圍聚在監獄外面。這天與第一批清教徒移民抵達新世界殖民地，已相隔二十年。

「良善的婦女們，」一名婦人大聲說道：「要是由我們來定賀絲特・普林這種邪惡女人的罪，那她得到的刑罰，才不會像城上法官們所判的那麼輕！」

「是啊！」另一名婦人附和道：「他們最起碼也應該用熱鐵烙印在她額頭上！把印記做在她前胸衣襟上的話，她隨時都可以遮掩起來了呀！」

「就是啊！」又一位嚷嚷道：「她呀，即使想隨心所欲的遮掩，烙印仍會永遠存在她心裡的！」

接著，佈滿鐵刺的監獄大門霍然打開。大門內的陰暗處，浮現出一個碩大、駭人、一身黑衣的人影。他伸手要將一名年輕婦人推送出來，但婦人推開他的手，帶著尊嚴，自己邁著步伐，步入天光下。

p. 16–17 婦人的懷裡，抱著一個三個月大的嬰兒。嬰兒眨著眼睛，因為這是她頭一次感受到陽光照在臉上。婦人站在市民完全看得清楚的地方，將懷裡的嬰兒低低抱在臂膀裡，露出她的衣裳。她面泛紅霞，卻掛著驕傲的微笑。

她前胸的衣襟上，有一個斗大的字母A。這個字母是拿細緻的紅布，用鮮亮的金線鑲繡而成，圖樣設計雅致而別出心裁。

賀絲特‧普林是個身材高挑的年輕婦人，她體態高雅，有著一頭烏亮亮的秀髮。那些認識她的人，都很驚訝她在這樣的處境下，還能顯現出美貌與淑女儀態。

「她的針黹手藝的確高超。」一名婦人評論道：「可是以這種方式來展露，多丟人啊！」

「以吾王之名，讓路！」獄吏吆喝道：「從現在到中午，人人都有機會把這個壞女人看個清楚。過來，賀絲特，到市場去將妳的紅字示眾！」

p. 18–19 圍觀者讓出一條窄道。賀絲特‧普林走向公開受懲的指定區。她鎮定地來到市場的西緣，緊鄰著波士頓最古老教堂的那座刑台。刑台是一座平台，用來公開執行刑罰，以做市民使之遵守法律。

刑台上有一具示眾枷，那是設計來夾緊人頭，使其任憑公眾注視用的。但是賀絲特‧普林並未被判受這樣的桎梏，她的刑罰僅為在刑台上站立三個小時。

她登上階梯，開始接受刑罰。觀眾肅靜地盯著她和那個紅字。賀絲特已經做好心理準備，來面對公眾恥笑和侮辱的攻擊，然而她卻發現，人們凝重的靜默，更教人難以忍受。

她站在刑台上，隨著回憶的浮現，她想起了自己的種種。她可以看到、感覺得到她快樂的童年歲月。接著，她看見自己正對著鏡子凝視的臉孔，臉上散發出青春美貌的光彩。

　　然後，她看見一張年紀比她大了許多的男人的臉孔。男人的眼睛黯淡無光，皮膚因長年埋首研讀而顯得蒼白，他的身形略有缺陷，左肩微高於右肩。

p. 20-21　而後賀絲特‧普林的回憶終止。她發覺自己回到了刑台上，四周圍滿了市民，人們仍盯著她和她胸前的紅字。她垂眼看看胸前的字，摸摸它，好跟自己確定它是真實的。它的確是真實的，連嬰兒和她灼燒的羞辱也是真的。

　　在刑台上站了一陣子之後，賀絲特在群眾的邊緣，看見一個她無法漠視的人。那是個白人，站在一個原住民旁邊。那白人身材矮小，滿臉皺紋，穿著一身混雜了文明與野蠻的服裝。

　　儘管他試圖掩飾他的身體特徵，但他的左肩還是明顯地比右肩高。就在她盯著他看時，嬰兒因為被她抱得太緊而痛得哭了，但是她似乎充耳未聞。

　　那個外地來的男子也回盯著賀絲特‧普林。起初他的目光心不在焉，但待他逐漸琢磨出她的處境，頓時一臉驚駭。

p. 22-23　「請問您，好心的先生，」男子對一位市民說道：「這名女子是什麼人，為什麼必須受到這種公開羞辱？」

　　「你一定是外地人吧。」市民回答：「住在此地的人，個個都知道賀絲特‧普林和她的醜事。她在狄默斯岱爾牧師的教堂信眾間鬧出了大醜聞。」

「沒錯，我是外地人。」男子回答：「我在南方被野蠻的異教徒俘囚了好長一段時間。請告訴我，賀絲特・普林這女子所犯的罪行。」

「這個女人是一位英國學者的妻子。他決定加入我們這個殖民地，便叫他妻子先過來。可是之後這兩年，這個男人毫無音訊，讓年輕的妻子受自己無知的見識所害。」

「啊，我明白您的意思了，」男子苦笑道：「那她懷裡抱的那個嬰兒的父親是誰啊？」

「這件事情大家心裡都很疑惑，」市民說：「但普林太太不肯說出那罪人的名字。」

「他的丈夫應該來此解開這個謎團。」男子說道。

p. 24–25 「是啊，要是他還活著，是該這麼做。」那市民認同道：「一般而言，這項罪的刑罰是死刑，但是法官們發慈悲，畢竟她的丈夫八成已經屍沉海底。只不過從今以後，她餘生都得帶著那個通姦的紅色印記。」

「這是睿智的懲罰，」陌生人說：「她的印記，將如同一場譴責罪衍的活佈道。只是，共犯沒有跟她一起站在刑台上，讓我很氣憤。不過他會被揪出來的，一定會的！」

陌生人步行離去時，賀絲特・普林的目光始終盯著他。她感到安心，因為有群眾在場，這樣她就不用單獨與那個男子碰面。

驀然，一個聲音將她從自己的思緒中喚醒。「賀絲特・普林，妳現在必須聽我言！」站在教堂旁邊露台上的是市長貝林漢，那裡是法官用來宣佈刑罰的地方。露台上除了市長和其手下，還有其他的仕紳貴冑。

賀絲特・普林面向露台。她剛才聽到的聲音是來自波士頓最年老的神職人員，教堂的主管牧師約翰・威爾森。

p. 26–27 「賀絲特‧普林，」老牧師繼續說道：「我跟你們這裡的狄默斯岱爾牧師說過，他應該要逼妳立刻說出那個惡人的名字，是那人誘使妳墮落至此。」

接著，貝林漢市長發言道：「仁慈的狄默斯岱爾牧師，身為她的牧者，你要為這個婦人的靈魂負責。你必須力勸她吐實，從而證明她的悔改。」

為了回應這番話，狄默斯岱爾牧師起身對群眾講話。這位牧師是個年輕的神職人員，畢業自英國一流的大學。他洪亮有力的聲音，以及令人佩服的智識，讓他在所服務過的殖民地區裡，備受尊敬與讚賞。

「跟這位婦人說說，弟兄，」威爾森牧師敦促道：「你是唯一能挽救她靈魂的人！」

狄默斯岱爾牧師望向刑台上的婦人，開口道：「賀絲特‧普林，妳已聽到仁慈的威爾森牧師所說的話了。我殷切勸妳，說出共同罪人的名字吧。說出來，會讓你們倆的心靈都得到平靜。不要因為對他有不當的憐憫或是心軟，而不肯說出來。」

連賀絲特‧普林懷裡的嬰兒，都被牧師洪亮有力的聲音所感動。嬰兒抬眼看著他，小臉蛋上掛著半喜半憂的表情。但賀絲特對於這番呼籲，只是搖頭以對。

p. 28–29 「婦人，切莫試驗神的慈悲的限度！」威爾森牧師帶著生氣的聲調，說道：「妳只要說出名字，就可以因為有所悔悟，而把胸前的紅字拿下來！」

「休想！」賀絲特‧普林喊道。她深深凝視狄默斯岱爾牧師的眼睛。「這個字烙印在我心頭太深了，不是說拿下就能拿下的。我希望能把他的痛苦，連同自己的痛苦，一併承受下來！」

「説！」刑台周圍的市民們叫喊道：「説出嬰兒父親的名字！」

賀絲特在群眾嚴厲冷酷的聲音中，認出了某個聲音，她面色變得蒼白。但她仍執意説道：「我不會説的，我的小孩永遠不會有一個塵世上的父親，她只會有天國裡的父親！」

「她不肯説出他的名字，」狄默斯岱爾一邊喃喃低語道，一邊彎腰靠在露台上，手捂著心口。「她不肯説！」他對群眾宣布。

p. 30-31 一回到監獄裡，賀絲特就陷入神經質的歇斯底里狀態中，嬰兒也不停地嚎啕大哭。獄吏布瑞克特大人不斷留意她的情況，以確認她沒有傷害自己或是嬰兒。最後，獄吏帶了一位醫生來看她。這位醫生正是她在刑台上受罰時，對她起了興趣的那個陌生人，名叫羅傑・齊林沃斯。

獄吏領著他進入牢房，當賀絲特・普林一看見他，整個人都僵住了。

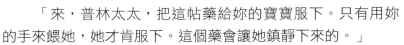

「不用擔心，」醫生向獄吏說道：「我會悉心照顧普林太太和她的孩子，您的監獄很快就會恢復安寧了。」

醫生以他從印地安人那兒學來的療法，用當地的植物調製了一帖草藥。

「來，普林太太，把這帖藥給妳的寶寶服下。只有用妳的手來餵她，她才肯服下。這個藥會讓她鎮靜下來的。」

賀絲特推開他的手，「你會不會毒害這無辜的嬰兒，來為自己報復？」

「婦人，別這麼可笑！」醫生以一種冷漠卻安撫的態度回答道：「我不會傷害這個不該出生的可憐嬰兒。」

婦人猶豫了一下，她把藥汁餵給嬰兒喝，嬰兒一下子便安祥地睡著了。

p. 32–33　之後，醫生也給了賀絲特些許藥汁，來安定她的情緒。她小心翼翼地看著杯中物，說道：「我怎麼知道你不會為了報復，就用毒藥來害死我？」

醫生回答道：「賀絲特，難道妳對我的認識只有這麼一點點，所以認為我的目的會如此膚淺？讓妳戴著胸前那個赤灼的羞恥活著，不才是最好的報復嗎？」

她聽了之後，淡淡地笑了笑，便把藥服下了。醫生趁她的藥漸漸起作用時，繼續說道：「妳知道的，我早該料到會發生這種事。我們結婚當天走在教堂走道上時，我就該看得見，這個紅字在走道盡頭閃耀。」

她向他說道：「你知道的，我一向誠實對待你。我始終跟你說，我對你沒有愛情，也不曾虛情假意。但我很抱歉，讓你很委屈。」

他回答：「不，我們都讓彼此委屈了。妳正值青春年華，我不該故意讓妳和我這個上了年紀的人結婚的。我們之間的關係很不平衡。不過，我去會找出那個懦弱的男人來報復，他丟下妳一人，讓妳獨自承受羞辱。雖然妳不肯告訴我他的名字，但我會把他揪出來，我一定會的！現在我只要求妳，不要讓這個鎮上的人知道我就是妳的丈夫，也不要讓那個我將報復的男人知道。」

「我不會說的，就像我不會把他抖出來一樣。」賀絲特說。

[第二章] 賀絲特的珍珠

p. 36–37　在與醫生談話過後不久，賀絲特‧普林的監禁期便結束了。然而，她生活在市民之中的煎熬，才剛要開始。

賀絲特可以自由地離開波士頓，但她決定要留下來，面對她的終身刑罰。她帶著她的寶寶，搬到市郊的一間小木屋。她靠著精湛的針黹手藝，得以謀個像樣的生活。她自己的開銷很省，但讓小女兒穿得很好，然後把多餘的錢捐作慈善。

由於她卓越的針黹手藝，市民們總是僱用賀絲特來工作。然而，他們用目光和言語，從不讓她忘記她的羞恥。

賀絲特的女兒名叫珍珠。取這個名字，並不是因為珍珠的美麗或價值，而是因為它昂貴的代價。

不過，嬰兒很快就長大，變成一個漂亮卻奇怪的孩子。賀絲特看著女兒，察覺到小女孩行為奇特。她擔心孩子似乎跟那個紅字產生連結，而被影響了。

p. 38–39　隨著珍珠漸漸長大，有件事越來越明顯，那就是無法強迫這個孩子接受規範。她不會理會母親最簡單的吩咐，而且性情不定，就彷彿賀絲特靈魂裡的戰爭，在珍珠的身上延燒著。

賀絲特很高興看到珍珠跟別的小孩一起玩耍，但珍珠卻跟母親一樣，是個被社會驅逐的人，而且她從很小就接受了自己的處境。

命運在珍珠的四周築起了一堵衝不破的圍牆。當她遇到鎮上那些惡毒的清教徒孩童時，他們會把她團團圍住，她就會變得很粗暴，拿石頭扔他們，像個小野蠻人般地尖叫。

看見女兒好鬥的模樣，賀絲特不禁跪下，向天父問道：「親愛的天父啊，我給這世界帶來了一個什麼樣的人啊？」

每當小珍珠聽到母親這樣吶喊時，她就會望著母親，然後人小鬼大地笑著。

珍珠最奇特的行為之一，發生在她還是嬰兒時。和其他大部分的嬰兒不一樣，她最先感興趣的，並不是母親的微笑；相反地，最先吸引她的，是母親胸口的紅字 A。

p. 40–41 幾年後，珍珠已經可以到處跑了。一天，她採集了一束野花，然後開始拿野花投擲在母親胸前的紅字上，而每當有花擲中紅字時，就開心得手舞足蹈。

賀絲特最初的本能反應是要舉起雙臂遮住紅字，但她忍住不動，讓花朵擊中心口，把疼痛當作是懺悔的一部分。看著母親顯而易見的疼痛，珍珠只是哈哈笑著，兩眼閃動著魔鬼般的微光。

「妳真的是我的孩子嗎？」她開玩笑地問著：「是誰創造妳的？誰遣妳來這兒的？」

「妳告訴我啊，告訴我啊。」珍珠回答道，變得非常正經。

「是天父遣妳來的，」賀絲特停頓了一下，回答道。

但是她的遲疑，並未逃過珍珠的鬼靈精怪。珍珠喊道：「祂沒有遣我來，我沒有天父！」

賀絲特喊道：「喔，求求妳，千萬不可以說這種話，祂創造了我們所有的人啊！」

「不，妳一定要告訴我，告訴我！」珍珠哈哈笑著，開心地跳來跳去。

賀絲特打了個寒顫，無法回答她的問題。

p. 42–43 一天，賀絲特帶著珍珠一起去貝林漢市長府邸。她告訴珍珠，她們要送回市長要她繡的一副手套。但是真正的原因，賀絲特聽過傳言，説是市民們正在計劃要把她的女兒從她身邊帶走。

他們懷疑珍珠可能是魔鬼的孩子，所以計劃把她帶走，以挽救賀絲特的靈魂。賀絲特還聽説，貝林漢市長是這項計畫的首腦，因此決定要找他談談。

這一天，她給珍珠穿上一件用金線繡成的亮紅色洋裝，配色設計就像她的紅字 A，讓孩子看起來就彷彿是紅字一個活生生的延伸。

當她們抵達豪華的府邸時，珍珠看見一叢盛開的玫瑰，便要求母親摘一朵紅玫瑰給她。

p. 44–45 賀絲特不答應，珍珠一陣嚎啕大哭，發出刺耳的尖叫。不過當她看到一些人走過來時，就突然安靜下來了。

那一群人是貝林漢市長、威爾森牧師、年輕的亞瑟‧狄默斯岱爾牧師，以及羅傑‧齊林沃斯醫生。狄默斯岱爾牧師最近健康情況不佳，而治療他的齊林沃斯醫生，已成為常和他在一起的親近同伴。

市長看到一身艷紅的小女孩，驚訝地問道：「這個小娃娃是誰啊？」

「啊，這是薄命的賀絲特‧普林的女兒，我們最近談的就是她。」威爾森牧師説道。

貝林漢市長説：「那好，我們就在這兒立刻審查這個問題吧。賀絲特‧普林，」他直視著她胸前的紅字，説道：「關於我們是否有責任要保護妳們母女的永恆靈魂一事，我們已經過廣泛討論。妳難道不認為，把這個孩子帶走，給她樸素的穿著，教導她天堂與俗世的真理，才是對她最好的嗎？」

「我比其他任何人更能教好我的女兒，」賀絲特・普林說著，把手指擱在她的紅字上，「我從這個學到了教訓。」

　　市長說：「婦人，那是妳的羞恥標記，也是我們認為最好把孩子交給有德之士的原因。」

　　p. 46–47 賀絲特・普林鎮定地說：「儘管如此，它給了我教訓，而這些教訓會使我的女兒更有智慧，更好。」

　　「這一點由我們來做評斷。」貝林漢說。之後他坐到一把椅子上，想把珍珠放在他的雙膝間，但是這孩子除了母親，不習慣和任何人觸碰，便逃開了。

　　威爾森牧師以善於跟兒童相處而著稱，他接續進行查問：「珍珠，妳可不可以告訴我，是誰創造了妳？」

　　有關清教徒對於人類靈魂之創造的信仰，賀絲特・普林在家裡教過她，但是珍珠決定要惡作劇地回答這個嚴肅的問題。於是她說，她不是在天堂裡被創造出來的，而是從監獄大門旁的那一叢野玫瑰中被摘下來的。

　　「這太可怕了！」市長喊道：「這個三歲娃兒，竟然弄不清是誰創造她的！」

　　賀絲特・普林一把將珍珠抓入懷裡，「神賜給我這個孩子，以回報祂從我這兒奪走的一切。她是我的快樂，也是我的折磨！我寧死，也不會讓你把她從我身邊奪走！」

　　「孩子，」老牧師威爾森說道：「珍珠會得到的照顧，要比你所能給的更好啊！」

　　p. 48–49 「神是把她賜給我保管的！」賀絲特・普林尖叫，然後轉向年輕的狄默斯岱爾牧師，喊道：「你替我說啊！你是我的牧者，你負責我的靈魂！你比這些男人更能了解我！別讓他們把她從我身邊奪走！」

「她的話中有真理。」狄默斯岱爾牧師用洪亮而顫抖的聲音說道:「神將這個孩子賜予這個母親,是要教她改掉她的邪行。母女關係是神聖的,我們是何許人,怎麼能說神把這孩子賜給她是做錯了?我們是何許人,怎能奪走慈悲的天主給予她生命中唯一的賜福?」

「說得好。」威爾森牧師說道:「那你怎麼說呢,貝林漢市長?這位賢明的牧師已經代表賀絲特‧普林,做了令人信服的答辯。」

「的確令人信服,」市長回答:「珍珠將留在她母親身邊,我們不會再對這個問題加以非議了。等長大了些,教會執事務必讓她去上學和上教堂。就這樣決定了。」

這時小珍珠抓起狄默斯岱爾牧師的手,放在她的臉頰上。牧師環目看了看,然後親吻了一下她的額頭。

p. 50–51 「真是個奇特的孩子,」齊林沃斯醫生說道:「或許我們研究她的個性,就能夠猜出她負罪的父親是誰。」

「那樣做是罪惡的,」威爾森牧師說:「最好還是為這件事祈禱,把問題交由神的意旨來決定吧。」

問題解決了之後,賀絲特‧普林帶著珍珠離開府邸。在府邸外面,她們遇見了貝林漢市長刻薄的姊姊,西本絲女士。這位女士在數年後,因為施行巫術而遭到處死。

「噓噓,」她發出嘶嘶聲:「妳們兩個,今晚要不要跟我們去森林,參加撒旦的聚會?」

「我們不要!」賀絲特‧普林回答:「我要待在家裡陪我女兒。但是如果他們把她從我身邊奪走,我就會跟妳去,用我自己的血,在邪惡的撒旦名冊上,簽下我的名字!」

經過這個事件之後，可以說，即使當時珍珠還那麼年幼，但是這孩子已經把賀絲特·普林從撒旦的陷阱中救了出來。

p. 52–53

清教徒與移民新大陸

新大陸移民來自英格蘭，這是大多數美國高中生學到的，但這並不全然正確。這些新大陸移民其實多數來自荷蘭，他們是在離開英格蘭之後，在荷蘭待了一段日子。

這些新大陸移民是清教徒，他們主張人人都應受高等教育，而且人人都可以在教會中獲選擔任高位。而英格蘭君主體制不樂見這樣的主張，因為它其實類似民主政府體制。

然而，這些清教徒並沒有政治意圖，他們比較關心於遵照嚴格而貞潔的教規過日子。這些清教徒離開英格蘭前往荷蘭，但是他們也不喜歡那兒的生活。他們擔心荷蘭人的影響力，會腐化清教徒團體內意志較軟弱的成員。

他們想住到一個僻遠的地區，在那兒他們不僅可以自由地過他們認為合宜的生活，而且可以控制其他人，使其他人也遵循嚴格的清教徒生活方式。來到新大陸之後，他們成功地創建了這種類型的社會，而這就是《紅字》的背景。

事實上，在這些清教徒移民抵達新世界的許多年後，他們的思想仍被當作美國建國的基本思想中的一部分。

［第三章］報復

p. 54–55 大約就在羅傑·齊林沃斯在城內擔任醫生並且住下來的時候，年輕的狄默斯岱爾牧師的健康情況開始變差。市民將牧師的罹病，和醫生到來這兩者之間的巧合，視為神的意旨與神蹟。市民長者認為，將狄默斯岱爾牧師的健康，轉移到齊林沃斯醫生手中，就是神的意思。

不久，這兩個人就常常在一起。狄默斯岱爾牧師對齊林沃斯這位長者醫生所擁有的豐富閱歷，深感佩服；而醫生則努力要找出牧師的病因。齊林沃斯確信，牧師的生理疾病，肇因於心理上的苦惱，但他想不出來牧師究竟為何所苦。

不久，他們搬到一棟屋子一起住。然而，隨著時間流逝，市民們開始對齊林沃斯醫生改觀。自從他遷入城中，他的外貌和舉止態度顯著地改變了。

他以前冷靜而和善，如今卻可以在他的臉上看到邪惡。謠言在城裡傳開，說牧師健康不佳，是撒旦所造成的，而撒旦正化身成羅傑・齊林沃斯來糾纏牧師。

p. 56–57 一天，牧師去醫生的實驗室看望他。醫生常常在實驗室裡，用他採集來的植物製作草藥。當時，醫生正在檢視一束不起眼的植物，那是從屋子旁邊的墓地採集來的。

「我就在那邊那一片墓地上，發現了這種葉子，」醫生指著窗子外面，說道：「這個植物種類我還沒見過呢。我發現它們從一座無名墓裡長出來，我懷疑是從那位男性死者的心臟裡長出來的。說不定，這代表了有一個可怕的祕密，和他一起被埋葬了。要是他在生前能坦承那個祕密，那情況就會好多了。」

「或許他也想要坦承，只是有口難言，」牧師說道。他緊抓著胸口，好像胸口在椎痛著。「我的教堂信眾在告解了自己的罪惡之後，都能大大地得到紓解。」

就在這時，醫生和牧師看到賀絲特‧普林和珍珠走在一條穿越墓地的走道上。珍珠很沒規矩地一路從一座墳頭跳到另一座墳頭，然後從一株牛蒡樹上摘了一把有刺的刺果，再把它們沿著母親的紅字 A 輪廓，黏貼上去。

p. 58–59 「啊，那個孩子不懂得尊重法律或權威，」羅傑‧齊林沃斯說道：「就在前幾天，我看見她把馬水槽裡的水，潑到市長身上。主啊，她到底是有什麼毛病？」

這時珍珠突然奔到窗前，朝狄默斯岱爾牧師扔了一顆有芒刺的刺果，然後哈哈笑了起來，對母親喊道：「我們走啦，母親，不然魔鬼會來抓妳，就像他已經抓到了牧師那樣啊。快來呀，否則他會抓住妳的！不過，他抓不到我！」

「你想，賀絲特‧普林把紅字所代表的羞辱掛在胸前，而不是藏在心裡頭，這樣是不是比較沒那麼悲慘？」就在母親帶著小女孩步行離開窗前時，醫生這樣問牧師。

「是的，我想是的。」牧師回答：「不過，我現在其實想談的是我的健康情況。對於我的慢性痼疾的病因，你的診斷是什麼？」

醫生說道：「坦白說，我想要知道，你是不是有什麼祕密沒有告訴我。你已經把你問題的一切都告訴我了嗎？」

p. 60–61 這番詢問式的刺探，顯然讓牧師慌張失措了起來。「這……我當然都告訴你了。」他結結巴巴地說道：「當然，我的靈魂裡有些部分，是永遠不能暴露給塵世間的醫生知道的。」

「可是如果你沒有敞開你的心靈和靈魂，我又怎麼可能治好你的身體？」

牧師聽到這裡，突然一陣憤怒，他把醫生的手推開，比了個狂亂的手勢，然後怒沖沖地衝出房間。

　　不到幾個小時後，牧師回到醫生的實驗室，為自己發了脾氣而道歉，然後兩個人很自然地就重拾友誼。

　　然而，這天稍晚時，醫生趁牧師坐在椅子上睡著時，悄悄溜進他的房間。醫生把手放在睡著的牧師的胸口，掀開他的襯衫，看他裸裡的胸部。而醫生因眼前所見，顫慄了片刻。隨後，他臉上露出得意而滿足的邪惡表情。

　　這天過後，羅傑・齊林沃斯與亞瑟・狄默斯岱爾的關係，起了微妙的變化。醫生依然保持他冷靜的外表，但私底下，他控制著牧師，並且計劃著報復他。

　　p. 62–63 狄默斯岱爾經常為了自己所犯的罪行，偷偷地懲罰自己。他會強迫自己不吃不睡，甚至會鞭笞自己直到流血。而後有一個晚上，他想到一種自我懲罰的新方法。

　　三更半夜時，他穿上衣服，悄悄離開屋子。

　　彷彿走在夢境中似的，牧師來到市場的西端，來到七年前賀絲特・普林曾經站在上面的刑台。

　　在那個漆黑的五月夜晚，牧師登上刑台的階梯，站在上方的刑台上。他覺得整個城鎮都在沉睡中，他不會有被任何人發現的危險。

　　而當他站上那裡以後，他的心靈被恐懼所吞噬。他感受到紅字從他的胸膛內，向外灼燒，這是他痛苦和疾病的根源。接著他會突然發出一聲嘶喊，叫得又長又大聲，以為全鎮的人應該都會被吵醒，然後跑過來看到他站在這個羞恥的地方。

　　但是睏倦的市民，只當他的嘶喊聲是野生動物在嚎叫，或是女巫的咯咯聲，因而沒有人跑過來看。

p. 64-65 之後，牧師覺察到一盞燈光從遠處接近。當燈光接近到可以辨認掌燈人時，牧師看出對方是威爾森牧師。但老牧師並未發現到年輕牧師，只是逕自走過。牧師知道，老牧師是去市長溫斯洛普的臨終病榻守夜回來，老市長大概剛過世。

老牧師經過之後，又有一盞燈光接近。這一回，牧師看得出來那是賀絲特·普林和珍珠。

「賀絲特·普林，」牧師說道：「是妳們嗎？」

「狄默斯岱爾牧師！」賀絲特驚呼道。看到他暗夜裡站在刑台上，她很吃驚，「是啊，是我和珍珠，我們正從溫斯洛普市長的臨終病榻回來，去給他量了一件壽衣。我們正要回小木屋。」

「賀絲特和珍珠，上來這裡吧，」牧師說：「妳們倆都曾經站在這上面過，可是當時我並沒有陪著妳們。」

賀絲特牽著珍珠的手，悄然無聲地登上刑台的台階。黑暗中，牧師摸索到珍珠的手，握住它。一股嶄新的生命力湧入他的心臟，在他的血管中奔流。他靈魂的重擔，卸除了。

p. 66-67 「牧師，」小珍珠說：「明天中午，你會跟我和母親一起站在這兒嗎？」

「不會，明天不會，」牧師說：「但是將來有一天我會的。」

「那要什麼時候才會？」珍珠問道。

「在最後的審判日那天，我會跟妳和妳母親，一起站在天主的面前。」他回答。

聽到這裡，珍珠哈哈笑了起來。突然間，一顆流星閃現，照亮了夜空。在它散發的冷光中，佇立著戴著紅字 A 的賀絲特、一手捂著心口的牧師，還有兩手各握著他倆的手的珍珠。

當牧師將目光移回地上時，他看見珍珠正指著一個從遠處漸漸走近的人。隨著那個人越走越近，他們看出那是羅傑·齊林沃斯。

「賀絲特，那是什麼人？」牧師說道：「我漸漸害怕他了，我已開始憎恨他！」

「我可以告訴你，他是什麼人。」珍珠說道，然後她嘴唇湊到牧師的耳邊，悄聲說了些胡言亂語，然後放聲大笑。

「孩子，妳是在嘲弄我嗎？」牧師問道。

「你不是真心的，」小女孩說：「你不肯明天中午跟我和母親一起站在這兒！」

p. 68–69 「尊貴的先生，」來到了刑台前的羅傑·齊林沃斯說道：「深更半夜的，你跑到這外面來，到底要做什麼？你是在夢遊嗎？」

「你怎麼知道我在這裡？」牧師很害怕地問道。

「我並不曉得你在這兒啊。我剛離開老市長的臨終室，正要走路回家。你最好現在跟我回家吧，不然明天你會沒有體力講道啊。」

牧師說：「好，我跟你回去。」他驀然感到寒冷而沮喪，彷彿從夢中被硬生生地叫醒。

經過在刑台上那一夜之後，賀絲特·普林漸漸擔心牧師會失去理智。她記得數年前與羅傑·齊林沃斯的約定，也就是她會把他是她丈夫一事隱瞞起來。

但是現在她覺得是她的錯，沒有警告牧師，羅傑·齊林沃斯那可怕的意圖。她決心要跟齊林沃斯談談，告訴他，她無法再信守那個承諾了。她必須告訴牧師，究竟是誰在折磨他。

沒過多久，賀絲特就與齊林沃斯醫生談上話了。因為數日後的一個下午，她在樹林裡看見他正在採集植物。

「去吧，去玩，」她跟珍珠說：「我要跟醫生說話。」

然後她轉向齊林沃斯，說：「醫生，我有一件重要的事情，必須跟您談談。」

p. 70-71 「啊，賀絲特女士，」齊林沃斯掛著微笑說道：「我聽說，市議會也許很快就會准許妳把胸前那個紅字取下了。」

「如果我配得上摘下它，它會自己掉落。」她回答道，並發現到過去這七年的歲月，已經將齊林沃斯變成一個魔鬼般的人。她知道，他那種尋求報復的生命，必然會將他的身體、心靈和靈魂，都變得無比的黑暗。

「妳在我的臉上看見了什麼，為什麼神情這麼嚴肅？」醫生問道。

「看見了某種讓我想哭的東西，」她回答：「但是，我們還是談談另一個悲慘的男人吧。七年前，我答應過對你的真實身分保守秘密，不過我有義務要幫助那個正被你逐漸凌遲至死的男人。我必須告訴他你是誰，好讓他明白你為什麼要這樣折磨他。」

p. 72-73 「那個懦弱的教士，已經察覺我的影響力和我的詛咒，」齊林沃斯說：「他只是怕得不敢跟他自己承認罷了。妳真愚昧，竟然想要幫助像他這樣卑劣無恥的人。他遺棄妳們母女，這麼多年來，任由這個城鎮來擺佈妳們。」

「我必須幫助他，這個紅字指示我要這麼做。」賀絲特喊道：「我不會再保守你的秘密了。」

「那妳就去跟他說吧。」齊林沃斯說：「妳把妳的好心浪費在男人的軟弱與不堪上，我真可憐妳。」

「我也可憐你，」賀絲特回答：「我可憐你內心裡的仇恨，已經將一個有智慧的人，變成了一個魔鬼！」

賀絲特在溪邊找到了珍珠，她一直在那兒玩耍。珍珠在自己的衣裳胸前，編排了一個綠色的 A 字，酷似母親的 A 字。

「啊，我的珍珠，妳的綠色 A 字，和我注定要配戴的紅字，是不一樣的啊。妳可知我為什麼戴這個字？」

「我知道，」珍珠回答：「和牧師捂著胸口的原因是一樣的。」

[第四章] 樹林

p. 76–77 賀絲特仍然決心要把羅傑・齊林沃斯的真實身分，告訴給牧師知道。她知道牧師何時會步行穿過樹林，並在那天帶著小珍珠出發，去攔他的路。

她們進入樹林時，小珍珠喊道：「母親，陽光不愛妳啊！都是因為妳胸前的 A 字，陽光逃走躲起來了！」

「那妳最好快跑去抓住它啊！」她母親說道。珍珠著實抓住了太陽，因為她站到燦爛輝煌的陽光裡。

她們來到林子深處時，珍珠要她母親坐下來歇一會兒。

「說一個故事給我聽。」她命令似地要求道。

「要聽什麼故事啊？」她母親問道。

「跟我說說那個在樹林裡出沒的魔鬼的故事。他都帶著那本又大又重、用鐵環扣住的黑簿子呢。還要告訴我，他是怎麼使人用自己的血，在他的簿子上寫下自己的名字！妳遇過魔鬼嗎，母親？」

p. 78–79 「是誰跟妳說這些的？」賀絲特問道。

「昨天晚上啊，我們在妳守夜的那棟屋子裡時，那個老太太説的，她那時候以為我睡著了。她説，這個紅字，是魔鬼留在妳身上的印記。」

「妳要是之後不再束問西問的，我就講一個魔鬼的故事給妳聽，」賀絲特説：「我遇過魔鬼一次，這個紅字呢，就是他留下的印記。」

驀然，賀絲特聽到樹林中傳來腳步聲。

「珍珠，快去吧，去玩。我要跟那個朝我們走來的人談話。」

「他就是魔鬼嗎？」珍珠查問道。

「當然不是，傻孩子，他是牧師。」

「對耶。」珍珠説，她看著牧師正穿過幽暗的樹林走過來。「而且他的手還捂著胸口，因為呀，他在魔鬼的簿子裡寫下了名字，魔鬼就把印記留在牧師的胸口上了。可是，他為什麼不像妳這樣，把印記戴在外面呢？」

「好了，去吧，孩子！」賀絲特喊道：「要待在溪邊附近，不可以走太遠！」

珍珠自己唱著歌便離開了。賀絲特看見牧師沿著小徑走來，他的樣子看起來更虛弱、更消沈了。

p. 80–81 「亞瑟・狄默斯岱爾，」她揚聲叫喚他：「狄默斯岱爾牧師！」

「是誰在説話？」牧師緊張不安地回答：「賀絲特，是妳嗎？」

「是的，是我。」她回答。礙於身分處境，他們已超過七年沒有獨過了，現在見到彼此，是既緊張又快樂。

他凝目看著她，問道：「賀絲特，妳找到平靜了嗎？」

她沈沈地笑了一下，低下頭看看自己胸前的標記。「那你找到了嗎？」

　　「沒有，我只找到黑暗和絕望！我對我的信徒宣導貞潔，可是我知道，真正的我，是空虛而痛苦的。我感覺撒旦時時刻刻都在嘲笑我。」

　　「你這樣折磨自己是不對的，」賀絲特説：「你深深悔過這麼多年了，一定要學著讓罪惡隨著時間過去！」

　　「不，賀絲特，我不配穿這一身包裹著我的聖服。」牧師喊道：「妳能把 A 字戴在胸前是幸運的，我的印記卻是焚燒在我心底！我真希望有誰，讓我告白我真實的罪行！」

p. 82–83 「我就是那個人，也是你的共犯。」賀絲特説道，她掙扎著要將今天碰面的原因告訴牧師，「你還有一個可怕的敵人，他跟你住在同一個屋簷底下。」

　　「一個住在我屋簷底下的敵人？」牧師訝異地説：「妳這話是什麼意思？」

　　「噢，亞瑟，請原諒我。」賀絲特喊道：「許久以前，我答應了別人去隱瞞你。那個老人，也就是名為羅傑·齊林沃斯的醫生，他是我的丈夫！」

　　牧師臉上出現一陣可怕的激動表情，他跌坐在地上，把臉埋在手心裡。

　　「我早該知道的！」牧師呻吟道：「打從我遇見他的第一天，我的心就告訴我，他隱藏著一個可怕的祕密。我為什麼就沒想到呢？哦，賀絲特·普林！這是妳的錯！我永遠不能原諒妳！」他大吼道。

賀絲特‧普林伸臂環抱牧師，緊緊地摟著他。他的臉頰就靠在紅字上，他想要掙脱，但賀絲特不放開他。

　　「你一定要原諒我！」她一遍又一遍地説道：「你一定要原諒我！」

　　[p. 84–85] 「好，我原諒妳。」牧師輕聲喊著：「我們並不是世上最不可饒恕的罪人。那個老人的報復，比我的罪愆更邪惡。他冷血無情地一步步害死我，我們犯的過錯，不及他的惡。」

　　「是的，我們所做的一切是神聖的。我們發生關係時，就是這樣告訴過彼此的，」她輕聲喃喃道：「你忘記了嗎？」

　　「沒有，」他輕聲説：「我沒有忘記。」

　　這是他們生命中最晦暗的時刻，然而在此黑暗中，有一種魔力使得他們流連不捨。他們坐在幽暗的樹林裡，手握著手，親吻著。

　　「羅傑‧齊林沃斯知道妳會揭穿他的身分，」牧師説：「如今，他會在所有市民的面前指謫我了。」

　　「不，我想他不會向人們揭發你的罪，」她説：「他會找其他伎倆，來滿足他黑暗的報復慾望。你一定要遠離這個可怕的人！」

　　「沒錯，他是在害死我，」牧師歇斯底里地喊道：「可是我又能怎麼辦呢，賀絲特？請幫助我！」

　　[p. 86–87] 「大海引你來到這個新天地，就能渡你回去舊世界。你應該返回英格蘭，或是去德國、法國，甚至義大利。」

「可是我怎能丟下我在這裡的職守？縱使我的靈魂已經墮落，別人還是需要我的幫助啊。」

「要是你被自己的痛苦給壓垮了，那就無法幫助任何人了。你必須拋下這個地方，」她說：「未來可以是充滿成功的新機會的。怎麼做都好，就是不要坐以待斃！」

「噢，賀絲特，我要死在這裡。」牧師喊道：「我沒有那種體力或勇氣，冒著風險獨自回到那陌生冷漠的世界。」

這時，賀絲特以低沉的聲音，輕輕地回答：「你不會獨自一個人走的。」

聽到這裡，亞瑟‧狄默斯岱爾懷著喜悅和希望地看著她的眼睛。

「我們不要回頭看了，」賀絲特說：「逝者已矣。瞧！」

說完，她伸指解開胸前紅字的扣鉤，將它扔到溪邊的石頭上。紅字躺在那塊岩石上，宛如一顆被遺落的珠寶一般，熠熠閃閃。

p. 88–89 卸除了壓在心頭的羞恥與痛苦的重擔，賀斯特大大地吁了一口氣。感受到這股自由，她才恍然明白那擔子是如何沈重。賀絲特解開她的無邊帽，一頭烏黑美麗的秀髮披落肩上。這時陽光穿過樹梢，灑滿了樹林。

賀絲特用充滿喜悅的眼眸，再度看著牧師，說道：「現在你得去認識我們的小珍珠！你見過她的人，但還不真正了解她！她是個奇特的孩子，但是你會學著去疼愛她的。」

「妳覺得，她會想要認識我嗎？」牧師滿懷期望地問：「我一向很怕小珍珠啊。」

「啊，那太可惜了，」賀絲特回答：「她會很愛你的。她就在不遠處，我來叫她。珍珠！珍珠！。」

珍珠在遠處，採集鮮花要給母親。她聽到叫喚，便慢吞吞地朝他們走回來。

　　「過來，」賀絲特說道：「我要你跟牧師做好朋友。」

　　但是珍珠並沒有遵從母親的命令，這個孩子只是指著母親少了紅字的衣裳前胸，直跺著腳。

　　p. 90–91　「我明白了，」賀絲特說：「小孩子不喜歡看到熟悉的事物改變，一點點的改變都不行。她是在思念從一出生就看見在我身上的字。」賀絲特指向溪邊岩石上的紅字，說：「字在那兒，珍珠，快去拿來給我。」

　　「妳自己去撿。」珍珠回答。

　　被孩子弄得無奈，賀絲特嘆了一口氣，走到溪邊，將紅字重新扣在胸前。

　　「妳現在認得妳母親了吧，孩子？」她對她女兒說。

　　「認得了，妳現在真的是我母親了！」小珍珠說著，一蹦一跳地越過小溪，加入他們。

　　「過來見見他，珍珠。他要跟妳打招呼，他愛你，妳願意也愛他嗎？」賀絲特問道。

　　「他是真心愛我們嗎？」珍珠問道，慧黠地看著母親的眼睛，「他願意跟我們手牽著手走進城裡嗎？」

　　「現在還不行，孩子，」賀絲特回答：「但是，不久後他就會時時刻刻跟我們在一起了。」

　　「他會時時刻刻用手摀著他的心口嗎？」珍珠問道。

　　狄默斯岱爾被孩子的問題弄得侷促不安，他蹲下身子，親吻珍珠的額頭，希望軟化她對他的觀感。

但是當他的嘴唇一離開她的額頭，她立刻跑到溪邊，洗去額頭上的吻痕，彷彿那是骯髒的東西。接下來，當母親和牧師在討論著如何在不久的將來團聚的計畫時，珍珠都站在遠遠的一旁。

p. 92-93

《紅字》中的象徵

在《紅字》中，霍桑運用象徵來強化他的主要理念。全書最重要的象徵，當然是紅色字母 A 本身。這個字母代表「通姦」（adultery）， 明顯地象徵著賀絲特的罪衍。

然而，賀絲特驕傲地掛著這個字。隨著歲月流逝，紅字 A 的意義便產生變化。到最後，它可以被視為「能力」（able）的象徵。賀絲特的女兒珍珠，則是這紅色字母活生生的示現。她帶來麻煩，是賀絲特的懲罰，但另一方面，她又是一個天賜的福氣，給了賀絲特活下去的理由。

相較之下，紅字在珍珠身上幾乎毫無用處，因為珍珠代表的正是造成此罪的熱情。這也反映出，清教教義對賀絲特的「懲罰」是無用的。賀絲特不肯屈服於他們的要求，反而成為一個有自尊而獨立的女人。

另一個象徵是以流星的形式出現。當狄默斯岱爾與賀絲特和珍珠一起站在刑臺上時，流星照亮了夜空。就在他告訴珍珠，審判日來臨時，他會與賀絲特站在一起，這顆流星的光便向世人「披露」出，狄默斯岱爾是屬於賀絲特和珍珠這一家人的。後來我們發現，他其實正是珍珠的父親。

這些象徵是文學技巧，讓作者用來幫助強調主題。

［第五章］天啟

p. 94–95 離開樹林之後，牧師不敢相信他們的會面是真實發生的。他們決定，歐洲城市會是最佳落腳處，讓他們展開新生活。好巧不巧，波士頓港有艘船，預定在四天後啟程赴往舊大陸。賀絲特因為行善認識那艘船的船長，所以可以安排她、牧師和珍珠一起搭船離開。

當賀絲特把這個安排告訴牧師時，牧師喜不自勝，表示道：「多麼幸運啊，當選佈道剛好要在三天後發表。」

當選佈道是為了祝賀新任市長的宣誓就職，這對任何一個新英格蘭地區的神職人員而言，都代表著事業的巔峰。

狄默斯岱爾與賀絲特談過話後，在返家途中，他有一種體力無窮的感覺，這對他而言是很不尋常的。他發覺無論做什麼事，他都不會覺得累。

p. 96–97 終於，牧師沉浸在書房的安寧與幽靜中，他可以在這裡撰寫他最重要的當選佈道文稿。正當他潛心於這項重要任務時，敲門聲響起。

牧師說著「進來」，心裡卻憂懼自己將看見一個邪惡的人，而果不其然，是羅傑·齊林沃斯。牧師始終沉默不語。

「哈囉，牧師。」羅傑·齊林沃斯說道：「我想你會需要我的醫藥協助，這樣你才能把感情和體力，投注在撰寫當選佈道文這項艱鉅的工作上。」

「這一回不需要了，」牧師鄭重地說：「前不久我去樹林散步，給了我煥然一新的精神和體力。我不需要你的任何藥物了。」

他們都明白，他們已經不再是互相信賴的朋友，而是仇怨甚深的敵人。

「牧師，你確定你不要服用我的醫藥，來幫助你完成這一篇最重要的當選佈道文嗎？天知道，說不定明年你就不在這裡了，無法再寫另一篇佈道文呢。」

「是啊，神若俯允，我會在一個更美好的世界裡。」牧師回答：「但以我現在的身體狀況來看，我並不需要你的藥物。」

「唔，我很高興聽到你這麼說，」齊林沃斯醫生說。

p. 98–99 齊林沃斯醫生離去之後，牧師召喚僕人，要他送來一頓豐盛的食物。他狼吞虎嚥，像一頭好久沒有吃過東西的動物一般。之後他寅夜疾書，書桌上的佈道文稿，一頁一頁地完成，被扔到一旁，彷彿上帝的話正透過他的手，傳達了出來。

隔天早晨，牧師醒來時，筆桿仍夾在他的手指間，而令人驚嘆的是，佈道文已完成了。

新任市長就職當天，市場擠滿了市民，他們等待著看官員列隊經過，並聽牧師的佈道。賀絲特和珍珠也加入了人群。

她們周遭到處是慶祝活動、角力比賽和各種競賽。戒律嚴格的清教徒社區裡，擠滿了在規範內盡情歡樂的人們。

當珍珠問起牧師會不會來這裡時，賀絲特回答：「會，但是他不會跟我們在一起。而且，要是今天我們看到他了，也不可以跟他說話。」

羅傑‧齊林沃斯也來參與慶典。當賀絲特第一眼認出他時，他正與次日啟航歐洲的船長交談。

p. 100–101 當賀絲特與那位船長談話時，船長告訴她，齊林沃斯將跟他們同船航行到歐洲。聽到這個可怕的消息，她的心往下沉。看見齊林沃斯時，她覺得他的笑容隱藏著駭人的、不為人知的意圖，但是她沒有時間去思考船長說的這個驚人消息。

牧師要發表佈道的時間就要到了。她看見狄默斯岱爾牧師，卻覺得他彷彿變了一個人，一個她從來沒有見過的人。她感到哀傷，因為他好像是另一個世界裡的人。

之後，賀絲特看見了西本絲女士，對方問她最近是否在樹林裡與牧師碰過面。賀絲特否認了。但是西本絲女士接著又告訴她說，牧師曾經去過樹林，而且還在魔鬼的簿子上簽下了名字。她還說，魔鬼有他的法子，可以在那些不肯承認在簿子上簽了名的人身上留下印記。

對賀絲特‧普林而言，讓情況更糟糕的是，這項慶典引來了許多住在偏遠地區的人們。這些人圍繞著她，盯著看，對她的羞恥標記指指點點。

p. 102–103 這一天，賀絲特所感受到的痛苦，更甚於她第一天戴上這個紅字時的痛苦。只是沒有人知道，同樣的羞恥印記，也在聖人般的狄默斯岱爾牧師身上灼燒著。

就在此時，整個市場都可以聽到牧師洪亮有力而滔滔動人的聲音，從市場東端的一座高台上傳來。他深刻雋永的話語，使得人群一片鴉雀無聲。許多人說，他們以前沒有聽過像那天所聽到的那麼睿智、崇高又神聖的性靈演說。

站在高台上，透過一波波由神所指引而撼動人心的話語，狄默斯岱爾牧師達到了他最驕傲的榮耀顛峰。

而此時，賀絲特和珍珠卻站在舊刑台旁邊，羞恥的符號依然在賀絲特的胸前熾紅地灼燒著。

p. 104–105 牧師的佈道一結束，音樂便隨之響起。市鎮的上流仕紳父老們列隊走在一條步道上，穿過人群。

他們抵達市場西端時，人群響起一片歡呼聲。待喊叫聲停息，賀絲特才看見牧師，並且被他慘白的面色和虛弱的樣子，給嚇了一跳。彷彿他已把他的最後一絲精力，全部投注在那番撼動人心而崇高遠大的佈道上。

而現在，他就像個孱弱無力的人，幾乎連站都站不住。威爾森牧師趕忙來到狄默斯岱爾牧師的身邊，試圖攙扶著他的胳臂，深怕他會倒下，但是年輕牧師甩開了老牧師的手。他憑著自己的力量繼續往前走，步履就像個搖搖晃晃的嬰兒。這時，他已走到非常靠近舊刑台的地方。

群眾吃驚地看著他，心裡納悶他這種在塵世上的虛弱，不知是不是他神聖力量的另一種徵象。 突然間，狄默斯岱爾牧師轉向刑台，並且伸出他的雙臂。

「賀絲特，」他喊道：「我的小珍珠，來我這兒！」他臉上露出極度痛苦的神情。珍珠奔向他，伸出雙臂一把抱住他。而賀絲特，彷彿被一雙看不見的手強迫著，慢慢地走近他。

p. 106~107 賀絲特支撐著牧師的身體重量，小珍珠握著他的手，就這樣，他們一起登上刑台的階梯。

「你瘋了嗎？」羅傑‧齊林沃斯小聲地說道，他就站在他們附近，「別跟那對母女站在一起！你會玷污自己的好名聲，被扔進不名譽的坑穴裡！這樣往後我就幫不了你了！」

「哈哈，」牧師嘲笑著齊林沃斯，「魔鬼，這一回你太遲了。有了神的幫助，我現在就要逃出你的魔爪了！」

群眾在騷動中注視著站在刑台上的三個人，仕紳貴胄們想不透他這個舉動的意涵。

齊林沃斯跟隨著在後，宛如在他們登台演出的最後一幕罪咎之戲中，是來跑龍套的。他目光陰沉地看著牧師，說道：「你大可以踏遍人間，找一個藏身處來躲避我，只不過，並沒有一個什麼山高水低的地方，是你可以逃走的，除了這一座刑台。」

p. 108~109 牧師望向賀絲特，說：「這樣，豈不是比我們在樹林裡商量的計畫更好嗎？」

「我不知道，這樣我們可能都只有死路一條。」她回答。

「神會保佑妳和珍珠的，至於我，我是個垂死的人了，這是我接受我的羞恥真相的最後機會了。」

說完，牧師面對其他的神職人員、新任市長、仕紳貴胄和成群的市民。

「新英格蘭的人民們！」他用莊重而威嚴的聲音喊道：「看著我，一個可恥的罪人！七年前，當老市長質問賀絲特‧普林的共同罪人姓名時，我就應該站在這裡了！你們都看見過這個婦人所戴的紅字，但是在你們當中，有一個人的羞恥和醜行的印記，是你們未曾見過的！」

說到這兒，牧師虛弱得差一點倒下。但是他極力讓自己站直，並且向前跨一步，與賀絲特和珍珠分開。「現在，你們必須親睹神的偉大力量，和真正的羞恥印記。看吧！」

`p. 110–111` 牧師很快地將聖袍扯開，露出他裸裡的胸膛。群眾盯著描繪在他胸膛上的恐怖神意，個個驚駭莫名。牧師臉上露出勝利的神情後，隨即倒在刑台的地板上。

　　賀絲特雙手捧起他的頭，齊林沃斯則跪到他身邊，說道：「你逃過了我！你逃過了我！」

　　「我的小珍珠，」牧師對他身邊的孩子說：「妳現在願意親我了嗎？」

　　小女孩俯身向前，親吻了他的唇。因為這一吻，那從小就一直籠罩著她的悲傷魔咒，破除了。她的淚水滴落在父親的臉頰上。

　　「別了，賀絲特。」牧師說。

　　「我們不是要在天堂相會嗎？我們不是要一起共度永恆的生命嗎？為了這個，我們已經付出了足夠的代價。」她對他說。

　　「唯有慈悲的神才知道啊，」牧師說：「要是祂沒有領我來這兒，向這些人說出真相，我大概就永遠地迷失了。讚美祂的名啊！祂的意旨完成了！別了！」

　　牧師說完，便嚥下了最後一口氣。群眾一片靜默寂然，又驚愕又敬畏。

`p. 112–113` 隨著日子一天天過去，許多人還是在談論他們所看見印在牧師胸膛上的紅字，酷似賀絲特的那個紅字。

　　有的人認為，他是藉由可怕的自我折磨，來將它印在自己身上的。另外一些人認為，那是羅傑·齊林沃斯使用藥物和魔咒，將紅字加在他身上。還有一些人則相信，是神將紅字放在他胸膛上，以懲罰他的罪。

　　許多宗教權威人士替狄默斯岱爾牧師的人格作辯護，聲稱他的臨終之言，宣告了他在賀絲特‧普林和女兒這件事情上是無罪的。

　　他們說，牧師只是用他在塵世上的最後片刻，透過他自身的例子，發表了一篇動人有力的佈道。然而，在可憐牧師的悲慘經歷中，最凸顯的最終寓意，是「要忠實！要忠實！要忠實！」。

p. 114–115 羅傑‧齊林沃斯尋求報復的對象逝去了之後，這個老人就這樣衰萎到不成人形。他在那一年也去世了，留下巨額的金錢和地產給賀絲特‧普林的小女兒珍珠。

　　從那以後，珍珠和賀絲特消失了好一陣子，不知去向。而到最後，珍珠成了新世界最富有的女繼承人，賀絲特‧普琳回到她的小木屋，繼續過著她勤奮工作兼做慈善的簡單生活。

　　當她最後年老辭世時，她被埋葬在一坏沒有標記的墳墓旁邊。那一坏墳連同她的墳，共用了一塊空白的墓碑。若干年後，墓碑上神祕地出現了一塊雕刻的盾飾。如果去讀碑銘，可以看見銘文是：「在一片漆黑中，是紅色字母 A」。

Answers

P. 34 (A)
① - (e)   ② - (c)   ③ - (a)
④ - (b)   ⑤ - (d)

(B) ① (b)   ② (b)   ③ (a)

P. 35 (C) ① (b)   ② (c)

(D)
① sermon   ② spikes   ③ fanciful
④ merciful ⑤ misbegotten

P. 74 (A) ① F   ② F   ③ T   ④ T   ⑤ F

(B) ① (a)   ② (b)   ③ (a)

P. 75 (C) ① (c)   ② (a)   ③ (b)   ④ (a)

P. 116 (A)
① occupied   ② frame   ③ devoured
④ crowd

(B) ① F   ② F   ③ T   ④ T

P. 117 (C) ① (c)   ② (b)

(D) ① → ⑤ → ② → ④ → ③

P. 128 (A)
① A strange child that was suspected of being a demon. - (d)
② This person had a scarlet letter inscribed on his breast. - (c)

❸ This person was forced to stand on a scaffolding with her baby for three hours. - ⓐ

❹ This person sought revenge on Reverend Dimmesdale. - ⓑ

Ⓑ ❶ forefathers, utopian ❷ relieved, presence
❸ burst, scream ❹ drearily, bosom
❺ remained, speechless

Ⓒ ❶ Where was Roger Chillingworth before he came to Boston Colony? (d)

❷ What was one explanation for the scarlet A inscribed on Reverend Dimmesdale's chest? (b)

Ⓓ ❶ When Hester Prynne came out of the prison, she stood with strength and dignity. (T)

❷ Reverend Dimmesdale insisted that they should take Pearl away from her mother. (F)

❸ Roger Chillingworth was a kind old doctor, who never wanted to hurt anybody. (F)

❹ Reverend Dimmesdale said he could not remember the time when he and Hester Prynne sinned together. (F)

❺ Some people thought that God placed the scarlet letter on Reverend Dimmesdale's breast as a punishment for his sin. (T)

紅字【二版】
The Scarlet Letter

作者 _ 霍桑（Nathaniel Hawthorne）
改寫 _ Michael Robert Bradie
插圖 _ Julina Aleckcangra
翻譯 _ 王啥
作者／故事簡介翻譯 _ 王采翎
校對 _ 陳慧莉
編輯 _ 王采翎／黃鈺云
封面設計 _ 林書玉
排版 _ 葳豐／林書玉
製程管理 _ 洪巧玲
發行人 _ 周均亮
出版者 _ 寂天文化事業股份有限公司
電話 _ +886-2-2365-9739
傳真 _ +886-2-2365-9835
網址 _ www.icosmos.com.tw
讀者服務 _ onlineservice@icosmos.com.tw
出版日期 _ 2021年2月 二版一刷（250201）
郵撥帳號 _ 1998620-0 寂天文化事業股份有限公司

Adaptor

Michael Robert Bradie

Auburn University
(BA - Mass Communications)
a freelance writer

國家圖書館出版品預行編目資料

紅字 / Nathaniel Hawthorne 著；Michael Robert
Bradie 改寫；王啥翻譯. —二版. —[臺北市] :
寂天文化, 2021.02 面；公分. 譯自:
The Scarlet Letter
25K+寂天雲隨身聽APP版
ISBN 978-986-318-959-6 (平裝)

1. 英語 2. 讀本

805.18 109020847